Meb,

Please forgive my ~~...~~ ~~...~~
and I promise I will stick to the facts!
I hope you were still able to enjoy it.

Riverside

Riverside

by JR Culver

iUniverse, Inc.
New York   Bloomington

Riverside

iUniverse books may be ordered through booksellers or by contacting:

iUniverse
1663 Liberty Drive
Bloomington, IN 47403
www.iuniverse.com
1-800-Authors (1-800-288-4677)

Because of the dynamic nature of the Internet, any Web addresses or links contained in this book may have changed since publication and may no longer be valid. The views expressed in this work are solely those of the author and do not necessarily reflect the views of the publisher, and the publisher hereby disclaims any responsibility for them.

ISBN: 978-0-595-50099-4 (pbk)
ISBN: 978-0-595-49658-7 (cloth)
ISBN: 978-0-595-61375-5 (ebk)

Printed in the United States of America

iUniverse rev. date: 3/18/2009

This book is dedicated to both the memory of my mother, Rebecca Jan Williams, who was always of great inspiration to me, and Lawrence Wesley Culver, Jr. without whose life this book could not have been written.

Chapter One

It was a freezing cold, clear morning no better and no worse than any other February morning in this sleepy North Texas town. The clean-swept streets and small frame houses gave a sense of nostalgia even though most were not more than a few years old. In all directions, the Great Plains swept away as far as the eye could see. Well, what was left of the Great Plains. Overgrazing and fifty years of farming had taken their toll.

The paper boy had just started around his last corner on his last street. He was growing more anxious by the house and his aim was suffering accordingly. Billy Hartman's thoughts raced forward; soon he would be grabbing his squirrel gun and heading off to hunt with his cousins, Henry and Lawrence, or LW for short. The memory of yesterday's horrific event, which set off a torrent of curses from Lawrence's father, came rushing back. This caused a slight drop in his arm, which would seem incidental if it had not caused the paper he was throwing to rise slightly and gain elevation as it accelerated. The paper cleared Mrs. Hunt's rose bushes by a mere six inches, which in turn allowed it to hit Mr. Hunt squarely in the back of the head. The explosion of coffee and language was an event worth witnessing, had anybody been present. Billy continued on his offensive way, oblivious to the carnage left in his wake.

The floor boards creaked ever so slightly, traitors to this clandestine expedition. Lawrence choked back his frustration as he listened for breaks in the rhythmic breathing of his father and mother. Heading to the creek for some fun and adventure was an accepted if not condoned practice in his house. But to escape without the completion of his daily chores was flirting with disaster. After yesterday, it was not his fault that the horny toad got away; he fully expected to be bombarded with work—something no self-respecting eleven-year-old could tolerate. Besides, the wind had died down and the temperature had dropped, allowing for perfect hunting conditions. Billy and Henry were waiting, and hours of stomping through brush and creek bottoms awaited. The thought that Mr. West, owner and guardian of West Farm, would be out watching for the would-be hunters only added to his excitement.

Once beyond the inter encampment, he had only to secure a means of transportation, load his supplies, and ride off through the last of the Mexican picket lines. For today, he was escaping the deplorable Santa Anna, his trusty steed a Schwinn bike. His supplies consisted of a squirrel rifle, thirty rounds, food, and a sleeping bag.

His escape route took him down Riverside to Twenty-eighth Street and then north on Beach. His ride should take no more than fifteen minutes, provided that the Mexican Calvary or, worse still, Santa Anna himself did not awaken and give pursuit. Once on Beach, he soon left the signs of civilization behind and followed the road to its conclusion without incident.

The dirt path turned due west and led directly into camp. His two older cousins sat upon a fallen tree. Both were clad only in their underwear, and Billy had a plug of chewing tobacco he had obviously stolen from his father.

Henry looked up at Lawrence, and his words fired off like a shot. "It sure as hell took you long enough. I thought you were grounded for sure."

Lawrence smiled. "Nope, I just looked 'em in the eye and said how sorry I was. They felt so bad they didn't even make me do my chores."

"I'll bet they didn't," replied Billy with a knowing smile. Both boys were now turning a slight shade of blue, and an unannounced challenge had been made. Neither boy wanted to be the first to show weakness and admit that he was freezing.

Lawrence glanced at his friends and then the sun and decided he had time to await the outcome. Perching down, he began to load his rifle. He watched under knitted brows as Billy began to show a much darker blue and Henry a slight tremor in his hands. A little bell of worry, slight though it was, began to ring in his head. The thought that Santa Anna, better known to him as his father, might give pursuit caused his face to take on a look of pain.

"What's the matter, Lawrence? You constipated or is that rifle just too hard for you to figure out?" Henry asked slyly.

"Look, little boy blue, I ain't constipated and I can handle this or any other rifle better than both of you! The only thing I got on my mind is squirrels."

Henry swallowed his retort. He was more interested in getting his clothes back on than teasing Lawrence, even if he did have a hundred dollar name. Besides, what the other boy said was true. He could handle that gun.

"Aw hell, I am putting my clothes back on before I catch pneumonia again," announced Billy at last.

"About damn time," said a thoroughly frozen Henry.

With the challenge decided and both his cousins donning their clothing, Lawrence knew they could now get down to serious business. The first squirrel of the day let loose a barrage of chatter moments before the bullet found its vitals and sent it crashing to the ground twenty feet below.

Billy and Henry both gave an envious glance at their true-eyed cousin and headed off in different directions, seeking their own trophies.

The hunting expedition lasted for almost five hours and netted a whopping four squirrels and two rabbits. It was time to put out the trout line in the creek and settle in for a hot meal. As the boys reached camp, the conversation turned to their second favorite topic, baseball. It was, without question, the future of each of the three to become stars in the majors. It was their focus on this topic which allowed the otherwise suspicious hunters to walk into the trap.

Santa Anna had come and was waiting at the edge of camp. The cousins did the only thing there was to do: they ran. Billy started cussing Lawrence and grown-ups in general. Henry began to slow down and finally came to a stop.

"What's the matter? You hurt?" asked Lawrence.

"No, I just figured there weren't any use in running," replied Henry.

"What the hell do you mean?" demanded Billy.

"Look, did you guys see who the other two men with him were?"

"Yeah, one was your dad and the other I couldn't make out," answered Lawrence. "That's because he was back in the brush, but I saw his truck. It was old man West."

"You sure Henry?"

"Yep. And they got our camp, bikes, and dinner. If we don't go back, we get a night without food and covers and a blistering waiting for us in the morning. Besides, Mr. West will just wait until we are asleep and pour cold water on us or something like that." The hard truth slowly sank into them all. They had been caught, and there was no way around it.

The three figures walking slowly toward them made a sorry sight—heads hung low, feet dragging. Defeat surrounded them like fog. It almost made Lawrence Sr. feel bad enough not to whip the tar out of his son—almost.

After the whippings ended, the boys had to hand over their trophies and apologize to Mr. West, who in turn threatened to whip them himself if he ever caught them trespassing on his land again. That done, camp was rolled up and the three desperados were made to ride their bikes in front of Lawrence Sr.'s car all the way home. Entering town as captured horse thieves, displayed before the gallows, gave a lesson to all of their fellow comrades.

The following morning found Lawrence hard at work on his mother's flower garden. He had been awakened at daybreak, handed a shovel and hoe, and then sent to the garden. It was now almost eight in the morning, and relief was on its way, though the torture of work and his relief were hard to tell apart. It was Sunday morning, and church would soon beckon. As he thought of this, his shovel slipped momentarily and the rose bush was almost cut in two. To return the favor, the bush caught him on the side of the face and left a three-inch scratch. It was just his luck that Mrs. Gillem and her snot-nosed girl, Becca, happened to be walking to their car at that moment. The torrent of curses reached them just fine in the cold, clear, morning air. A shrill call from Mrs. Gillem brought his mother out of the kitchen door. The following conversation led, as always, to another spanking and two days added to his sentence.

Breakfast was a mixed blessing. The food prepared was excellent by anyone's standards, but facing his mother was enough to sour even the most hardy of appetites. His mother, to be fair, was a beautiful and kind lady. But through the eyes of LW, she seemed at that moment to be the Wicked Witch of the West. His father had engrossed himself in the *Star Telegram*, something Lawrence saw as a pointless hobby. Who cared what the weather was like in Houston or what some guy in New York said? That was all a million miles away.

His father informed them that some guy named Hitler had become chancellor of Germany. *Well bully for him*, thought LW. *Maybe somebody in the world can go hunting and not get grounded for it.* Lawrence Sr. related passages in the paper, as he did every morning, asking questions that he really did not want answers to. "Did you know that Japan's navy is bigger than our own or that they discovered more oil in the Middle East?" LW did not know where Japan was or what the Middle East was the middle part of. Breakfast was ended when his mother informed him that it was time to clean up and get ready for church.

Winter slowly gave into spring, and the new baseball season arrived. This was the pinnacle of the year for the boys, and they enjoyed it to the utmost. The only down sides in their eyes were school and church. Both of these events held great promise for excitement and as well as the pitfall of boredom and the trouble that followed it.

The school bell began to ring, and LW took his seat. He was, after all, Mrs. Davenports least favorite student. He waded through science and mathematics and even managed to get a few minutes of sleep in social studies. The welt on his hand still stung, and he thought Mrs. Davenport needed to find a way to wake up a person that didn't involve violence. After lunch, Lawrence began to feel the effects of the squash he had traded for. His intestines felt like they were twisting up inside him, trying to get out. He raised his hand as politely as he could, requesting permission to go to the restroom. His request was flatly denied. Now unbelievable pain began to rack his body. It was at this time that a rather ingenious plan crept into his innocent mind. Giving a long, careful look around, he began to inch his pile of books toward the edge of his desk. Timing was everything. At the exact second that his book hit the floor, he would let it rip. His slow push took the books to the edge of his desk and then began their inevitable tilt downward. Timing, timing … the books came down with a loud crash, scaring everybody in the room and forcing all eyes and ears to turn immediately toward Lawrence just in time to hear him relieving himself. It was not the quite whispering of expelled gas, but the rather loud trumpeting of an elephant reverberating through the room. His insides felt fine, but now his ear began to hurt badly, and the fact that Mrs. Davenport was pulling him by it seemed to be the cause.

Mr. Tumklin was in a foul mood. The slowly increasing heat brought on by Mother Nature and mothers in general seemed especially ruthless this spring. The commotion in the outer office only added to his condition, and the fact that it was LW caused his ulcer to act up. In fact, he blamed the entire existence of his ulcer on the voice that could be heard just outside his door. That boy had caused far more problems than any other child in the school, and this time he would learn his lesson. LW stood bravely before the principal and told his story—a good one, which he delivered like a true politician. When he finished speaking, he smiled and lowered his hands with a flourish, putting the final touches on what he considered his greatest speech to date. Had he been a little older, a little more experienced, he would have recognized the point at which he lost his audience. But LW seemed oblivious to the telltale signs, feeling safe and secure in his perfect story.

As Lawrence finished speaking, Mr. Tumklin slowly blinked and his eyes came back into focus. He was totally unaware of the majestic explanation that had just been laid out so eloquently before him. Instead, he had been dreaming of the perfect punishment, which he quickly shared with the beaming defendant.

LW spent the next hour and a half writing a letter of apology to everyone in class, including his teacher. Of course, he did this while enduring excruciating pain from the six licks he had received from a smiling Mr. Tumklin. In fact, LW was more than a little suspicious about that smile and the satisfied noise his punisher had made after the licks had been administered.

At that very moment, Mr. Tumklin had a dreamy smile on his face and his feet sprawled on his desk as he explained the bad news to Lawrence's mother.

LW could not wait for tonight's game and an end to his unjust punishment.

The White Socks led by a run, the bases were loaded, and it was the bottom of the seventh and final inning. The Panthers' best hitter was up, and everyone moved back. This was the second to the last game of the season, and the White Socks trailed first place by a game and a half. The first-place Indians had lost earlier that night, and a win would put the Socks half a game out with one game left, against the Indians. Their destiny was now in their own hands. It was do-or-die time. The first pitch was high and outside. The second pitch was a streamer right down the middle of the plate. The batter took a whale of a swing and sent a hard grounder toward the short stop. The third base runner began to head home for the tying run. The ball took a quick hop, and the short stop moved into a running dive, scooping the ball up as it hit the ground. LW made a quick roll and an awkward throw to first. The ball flew straight and fast toward Henry's outstretched glove. The runner and ball seemed to arrive at the same time. There was a momentary pause for effect, and then the umpire screamed, "You're out." Pandemonium reigned on the field and in the stands as players and parents alike heaped congratulations on one another.

If Lawrence had thought that last night's victory would earn him a moment's respite from his punishment, he was exactly right. Upon returning home from school the next day, his mother gave him a hug and a snack. Shortly after that, his reprieve was over and his mother gave him the mop. The insult could not have been worse; this was women's work. He began to mop slowly at first and then picked up speed, working feverishly. Five minutes later, he learned a lesson that all children must learn.

Punishment is not about the work; it's about the time. And so the house got a second, if not more thorough then at least a longer mopping. Dinner and homework soon followed. That night, while playing catch out in the yard with his father, who in his day had played baseball professionally, LW explained his well thought out plan of the day before. His father told him how inappropriate his actions were in polite society. Even though crude language and actions were acceptable for a hunting camp, they could not be tolerated in certain other circumstances. LW was a very thoughtful young man as he lay in bed that night, completely unaware that the laughter that was coming from his parents' room was in direct relation to his actions of the previous day.

The following day at school was uneventful, excluding the disgusted looks Mrs. Davenport gave him. Lawrence was so preoccupied with dreams of glory that that afternoon, he failed to cause even a single incident, which pleased his teacher greatly.

After school, Billy was waiting at the end of the block, glove in hand. Both were too nervous and excited to throw around their usual sarcasm. Tonight was the night. If they could just beat the Indians, all would be well and their summer would be set.

By game time, the stands were packed. Everyone knew what was at stake, and tensions were running high. The Indians were up first, and their lead-off batter took the opening pitch and sent it soaring into left field. The White Socks' left fielder arrived too late to make a play and so he got his glove on it and quickly relayed it in. A double off the first pitch of the day was a bad omen. The next five innings echoed that first pitch. By the bottom of the sixth, the Indians were well on their way to a league-winning victory. The score stood at 2–0, and the pressure was mounting.

LW led off, and the first pitch was low and outside. The second pitch was high and outside. A swing sent it sailing down the third base line, and it went foul. The third pitch was a chest-high fast ball, smoking over the outside of the plate. When the ball landed nearly eight seconds later, the score had been cut in half. The sole low home run had changed a disgraceful whipping into a ball game. The next batter up was Billy. He had been hitless all night, and LW, now self-confident, begin a mouthing that could be expected from him. "What's the matter, Billy, you nervous? If you are, your mamma is right behind you. Or maybe you need some batting lesson. Let me know cuz I'll give 'em to you."

Billy soon found himself in quite a dilemma; his desire to hit the ball was slowly being replaced by his stronger desire to hit his cousin. He was down to two strikes and one ball. There was no way he could strike out and face a smiling LW all summer long.

Melvin Tremer found himself in an unfamiliar situation. With his eighty-four-mile-per-hour fast ball, he was without question the premier pitcher in the league. By compiling six shutouts and three no-hitters, he was a shoe-in for league MVP, and he was about to hand his team the championship. Nevertheless, something was wrong; his arm had started to get a rubbery feel to it. If he could just strike out this red-faced kid, he would be all right. What he faced was a very determined and motivated batter.

For Billy, the urge to knock out his cousin was almost overwhelming. The image of LW lying flat on his back made him feel euphoric. Again and again, he managed to foul off Tremer's pitches, until finally, on the ninth pitch, he managed to send one sizzling down the third base line. His thoughts were so solidly on his cousin that for almost two heart beats, he stood at the plate, grinning. When he did remember to run, he made it all the way to second via a stumbling headfirst dive that left him covered with dust and bleeding from his nose. His safe emergence at second was greeted with cheers and loud, annoying laughs from his dugout. The author of these laughs happened to be the same individual that his increasingly sadistic thoughts were on.

The Indian's manager simultaneously made the correct analysis that his pitcher was tired and the wrong decision to begin to warm up his replacement. The next Sox's batter swung at a high pitch and gave Melvin a much-needed gift, a high infield fly. The short stop made quick work of the fly ball and tossed it nonchalantly back to Melvin. The all-star pitcher began to relax with one down and one stuck on second. All he needed was two more outs. As he wiped his forehead on his sleeve, he glanced at his dugout, and the sight that met him there stunned him to the bone. What he saw, of course, was Clyde Parsons warming up. Shock quickly faded to anger. He had never been pulled. His next three pitches flew with lightning speed. Three pitches, three strikes. Melvin was now one out away from ending the inning. The Indians' manager made his final mistake of the evening. With a three-pitch strike out, his pitcher gave him a false sense of security.

The next up to the plate was Henry. As Melvin let lose with his pitch, something let loose in Melvin's arm. A horrid look of agony perched itself on the face of both the Indians' pitcher and manager. One because of the pain in his arm; the other because of the pain of watching a forty-mile-per-hour pitch go in waist high and dead center. The crack of the bat echoed as the ball sped toward its destination some fifty feet beyond the center field fence. The noise level reached deafening proportions as the two heroes crossed home plate. Shortly thereafter, there seemed to be some kind of disturbance in the White Sox's dugout. To the casual observer, celebrations were under way, but a closer inspection would have revealed a fistfight that threatened to engulf the entire bench. It took a full three minutes for Billy's anger to be quenched; that and the fact that both his cousins now bled as much from the nose as he did finally brought order, and the game continued. Clyde Parsons threw a five-pitch walk and then got a slow grounder to second that finally ended the decisive sixth inning. Henry would take the mound in the seventh and final inning for the Sox. Nervous though he was, because should he fail he faced the same taunting summer his cousin Billy feared to face, he still pitched a good final inning. He got two fly balls and a grounder to crush the Indians' dream. Now summer could be faced with high hopes.

That summer was one of complete and utter pleasure, a summer that would never be surpassed, capped off with the entire family making a pilgrimage to the Grand Canyon, or as LW called it, "the biggest crack in the whole world." This trip was followed by countless baseball games and endless hunting trips.

The years slipped by as childhood years often do, too fast for the parents and too slow for the child. What is amazing is that all the characters in our story survived the next few years. And out of all of them, perhaps Mr. Tumklin was the most pleased and relieved to pass Lawrence on to high school and the next victim.

It is here, during these years, that our story truly begins. So LW began high school, totally oblivious to the coming and goings outside his little world. But fate and destiny were about to smash his small world head on, bringing him into the bigger world of politics, madmen, and their massive legions of hate.

Chapter Two

High school seemed to be nothing more than a repeat of previous years. LW, with Billy and Henry, seemed not one bit perturbed as he entered the doors of higher education. Most of the older boys had already felt the steel of his fist and had decided not to pursue any course that could lead to a repeat of previous episodes. So for the most part, it was business as usual for the trio—that is, until science class. LW entered the room in his usual loud and arrogant way. He looked around and then stopped dead still. This caused Henry to bump hard into his back and fall sideways, straight into Billy. Billy happened to be bent down, tying his shoe. The collision took both boys by surprise, and Billy, understandably, took the hit as a planned assault. During the entirety of the ensuing fight, LW never moved his eyes, which were locked onto the prettiest girl he had ever seen.

While his cousins were escorted to the principal's office for their first of many visits that year, LW took his seat without saying a word. In fact, he sat quietly during the entire class, with a perplexed look upon his face. He could not understand the strange and unfamiliar feeling that was now pulsating through his body. On one hand, the girl was an exotic creature; on the other hand, she was just a girl. As a matter of fact, he knew the girl from junior high; her name was Doris

Hunt. But something was very different about her now. It was as if she had undergone some kind of metamorphous during the summer break. For her part, Doris had noticed the attention that Lawrence was graciously giving her. He too was familiar, a mean, obnoxious boy with filthy habits and a loud, boisterous voice. He was the kind of boy her mother was constantly putting down. Doris Hunt was known for her gentle kindness, perfect ladylike manners, and incredible voice. Singing was her passion, and she saw herself becoming the star of an opera one day. She worked hard at keeping her reputation and manners intact. The knowledge that she would one day be a wife and mother gave her immense pleasure. But the look she was giving the nasty boy in front of her was anything but ladylike. Though she did not know him, she felt disgust and that somehow he was below her.

The class bell interrupted LW's thoughts, and given the nature of those thoughts, it was a good thing. He grabbed his books and joined his fellow students in a mad dash for the door. The first day of school was over.

It took all of one hour for LW to drop his books and change into shorts. The small but deep hole in the creek was his destination, and his cousins were probably already there. When he arrived, he found the hole empty and was a little confused by this development. But the water did look inviting, and he soon forgot the girl and his uneasiness. Whatever was holding up his cousins was none of his affair—that was until the other two boys entered the creek and begin to pound on LW. The fight was short-lived, mainly because the water made their blows ineffective and quickly tired the combatants out. After they explained about their first day of detention, LW awkwardly mentioned his thoughts about Doris. When he finished, the two boys stared for a full minute at their star-struck cousin. And then they began to laugh and laugh and laugh.

"Ha ha ha! LW has got himself a girlfriend," roared Billy.

"And a stuck up one at that," screamed Henry. And then the taunting began. "Lawrence and Doris sitting in a tree." That's all Billy got out before a mighty hammer slammed into his already tender mouth. Henry took a brave step forward to help his wounded pard but then noticed his red-faced foe had turned his anger towards him. Henry beat a hasty retreat, but to his horror, Lawrence proceeded after him, and a glance at his fallen comrade told him Billy was out of the fight.

Doris and her girlfriends were walking along the path that ran beside the creek, when a loud crashing noise, followed by cursing, interrupted their peaceful walk. Then a filthy, half naked boy burst from the line of trees and bee-lined for the group. The girls became concerned and began to talk nervously. Henry, out of breath and tired, looked up into Doris's face. This brought another round of screaming laughter from the boy. Half laughing, half choking, the boy stumbled off. More crashing brush and curses announced the arrival of another filthy, half naked boy. But this one was red-faced and clearly mad. His eyes quickly swept the group and lingered briefly on Doris before finding his intended prey. The girls, through some sort of natural herd instinct, moved away from LW, giving him a clear path to Henry. As he dashed by, he noticed a small log lying on the ground. It so happened that this log was about the size of a baseball bat. He hefted it, tested its weight, and then proceeded toward his cousin. Doris felt her disgust give way to alarm. Without a moment's hesitation, she stepped in front of LW.

"And just what do you intend to do with that stick?" she asked disapprovingly. LW, for the second time that day, was thunderstruck. Faced with the object of their disagreement, he just stood there, his mouth agape, staring. Doris patiently awaited his answer.

Finally, LW muttered, "I am going to bash him with it."

"Oh no, you most certainly will not," Doris snapped.

It was apparent that Henry had little faith in his savior's ability to persuade his cousin. He took advantage of LW's momentary pause to effect his escape. LW tore his gaze from Henry and looked closely into the eyes of this bold girl.

"Now give me that stick," demanded Doris.

"Hell I will," stammered LW.

"Mind your manners, you filthy boy."

LW was aghast at being called down by a girl. He stepped back and then, remembering his purpose, began a long circle around the girls. But before he got very far, he dropped the stick and then disappeared in the direction Henry had taken. None of the girls noticed the slight smile that glowed briefly on Doris's face. The girls began to talk quickly among themselves. Their musings were interrupted by yet another crashing in the brush, and out popped a bloody, dirty Billy.

"Evening, ladies. Did any of you happen to notice two other guys running by here?" None spoke, but Doris quietly raised her arm and pointed in the direction LW had taken. Billy muttered his thanks and then stumbled after his cousins.

Science class became the high point of LW's day. He could not put his finger on it, but the feeling was there just the same. His two cousins still snickered from time to time but wisely never mentioned it again. Most of their conversation centered around the recent depression, school, or school activities. The war in Europe was talked about more and more, but with a vague uneasiness.

Friday afternoon was a special time, with the pep rally followed by the football game. But this afternoon was abnormally tense. For in science class, they would dissect frogs, something most students found appalling. LW, Henry, and Billy were in good spirits. Finally they would get to do something fun. After all, they had been dissecting frogs for years and had eaten quite a few as well. LW practically ran to his science class and was sitting in his desk well before any of the other students arrived.

Once the bell rang, the classroom became as silent as tomb, and then the teacher came out of the back room carrying trays of dead, preserved frogs. *Ughs* and *ahhs* filled the room as the carcasses of frogs were slapped down with metallic thumps. Doris was in trouble. An honor student with straight As, she was about to vomit on her latest assignment. Her boyfriend, if you could call him that, showed absolutely no desire to help her. As the rest of the class began cutting and classifying, Doris sat staring at the horrid dead frog. The smell of formaldehyde permeated the air. She looked up at LW and could actually hear him whistling. She could not believe her ears; that gross, disgusting boy was actually enjoying it. He happened to glance up at that moment and saw the expression on her face.

"Is something wrong with your frog?" he whispered.

"Yes, it's dead and smells bad," she retorted.

"Well, would you rather it was alive and hopping around?"

"If I didn't have to cut it open, yes," she replied.

Lawrence moved quickly, slicing her frog from its throat to its privates. Then he quickly pinned the skin back and, with a sure flick of his thumb, laid bare the insides. He just as quickly removed parts and pinned them to the tray. Doris could not believe her eyes; that boy had just helped her. What was worse was that she had never cheated at anything in her life. While she began to wrestle with this, the teacher walked by and saw her handy work.

"I think the other girls in this class could use a lesson from Miss Hunt. She has already finished her work and didn't even complain or faint," the teacher stated. This extracted dirty looks from her girlfriends and snickers from the other boys.

At this point, Harold, Doris's so-called boyfriend, managed to cut his frog in two. It was really a remarkable achievement, and as the other boys marveled at his feat, they began to come up with original ideas themselves. One of those ideas soon took shape. The head of one frog quickly appeared stuck through with a number two pencil and found itself impaled in the ceiling, its eyes staring out and tongue dangling down. This brought tears of joy to Lawrence's eyes and loud laughter from Henry. Billy did not notice, for he was busy expertly skinning his frog. It was not long before frog parts were flying through the air and splattering on school books. The teacher was ready for this and began blowing on a whistle. Through this nonviolent method, she soon regained control of her classroom.

"Now, every person who is finished, please bring your specimens up here for disposal. But first I must visually inspect each tray to make sure that there are no missing parts." This brought pandemonium back to the room and required more whistling. As Billy set his tray down, his teacher glanced at it and then stopped and stood staring at it.

"All the pieces are there," Billy said defensively.

"Yes, I can see that, Billy. You go along now and I will take care of this," she replied absentmindedly. As Billy left the classroom, his teacher sat staring at a perfectly skinned specimen, with each and every part laid out. She could find no flaws. Not one organ was torn, cut wrong, or otherwise damaged. The skin lay beside the body, and it too was flawless. Never in all her years teaching had she ever witnessed something like this. After a moment, she picked up the tray and headed for the principal's office.

On the way to the pep rally, Doris caught up with Lawrence.

"I did not get a chance to thank you," she said shyly.

"You looked like you needed the help is all," he replied. "I would not call it a rescue, but you're welcome." With that, he turned and headed into the locker room, passing his cousins, who were suddenly occupied with their feet.

Lawrence played defense and loved to hit. Tonight, though, it was the other team doing the hitting, and the game ended 13–0. After they took their showers, the three cousins headed to the drug store for a root beer and a hamburger. Harold was there, and the three took up seats around him. Harold, who played tight end, and happened to be dating Doris, had the most to say. He went into every detail about the game. Every move, every play, was relived. After they got him to shut up, they began to get to the important subject: planning a hunting trip for the morning.

Billy noticed that LW barely participated in the conversation. LW was getting impatient waiting for Harold to mention Doris. Billy, who was enjoying his cousin's discomfort, finally inquired about her.

"Her parents wanted her home right after the game. But I plan to stop by there after I leave here," stated Harold.

"You know, Harold, it's not really dating if you never go on a date," Henry said. Everyone got a good laugh out of that—everyone except LW. He was staring intently at Billy.

"Say, you guys could help me," Harold said with an excited yelp.

"How's that?" asked Henry.

"I have been sorta going out with Doris for a while now. I have not even gotten a little kiss this whole time." LW thought that this was probably a good thing, but at least they were talking about the subject he was most interested in.

Harold continued, "Her parents won't let her go anywhere alone with me. So, I think the only place I could get a kiss would be on the front porch." The cousins were appalled at the thought of trying to steal a kiss right in front of her house.

Billy voiced his opinion. "If you do that, her parents will see you for sure and then you won't ever get to see her again."

"That's right. With that porch light on, they are bound to see me, and that's where you fellas come in."

"You need us to take out that light," Henry stated, seeing where the conversation was headed.

"You got it. It would be simple."

"If it's so simple, why don't you do it?" Billy asked.

"Cause if I do it before I knock, they will know something's up, and if she sees me doing it, she will go in. It has to seem like it just happened."

"I'll do it," LW said. "I can shoot that light out from across the street."

"No, I don't want it shot out. Just unscrew it," Harold said, a little shocked by the offer. He looked suspiciously at LW, finally deciding that he must have been joking.

"LW, if you help him, you leave your guns at home," Billy stated. He was under no illusions about the sincerity of LW's offer.

Harold was ready. He looked to make sure that his accomplice was adequately concealed and then knocked on the door. Everything went as planned. LW waited until Doris's back was turned and then quietly sneaked up and unscrewed the light bulb. He jumped back into the bushes and disappeared as though he had never been there. Harold moved quickly and crushed Doris to him in a desperate embrace. But instead of feeling her warm lips, he felt the stinging sensation of her hand as it slapped him on the cheek. She then turned and headed back into her house. Both boys retreated safely down the street, with LW snickering and obviously enjoying the anger that his companion felt. Now LW could enjoy his upcoming hunting trip with a clear conscience.

It was a muggy day to be out clumping through the underbrush in the Trinity River Bottom, but the squirrels could not wait, and so the hunters were obliged to join them. LW was in exceptionally good humor this fine morning. Waking up before everyone else gave him the opportunity to work on the problem that was slowly eating at him. That girl from class was as stuck up as anyone he could ever remember meeting—even more so than the ladies at church. But there was something about her that stuck a burr in his mind. True, he did cut up her frog, but that really did not mean much. Being an only child, and a spoiled one at that, LW had a disoriented view of women. The only ones he really had any dealings with were his own family, who fawned over him night and day.

Movement in the trees above slammed the door on any further contemplation on the light and dark sides of the female persuasion. The flip of a tail, the downward motion of a branch—all signs that this morning's prey were in sight. A few minutes of silent stalking brought LW to a tree just opposite the one the intended victim was currently occupying. He was taking careful aim and slowly squeezing the trigger when an even stealthier movement caught his eye. An old fish snake was slowly crawling out of the river in search of a bed. The strange thing about fish snakes is that some are diamond-backed. Now, any fool can tell the difference between a fish snake and a rattler—that is, any fool who isn't just waking from a sound sleep after a long night of frog gigging. And LW knew of just such a fool.

Billy was just starting to come to, with a happy and content yawn, a big stretch and … something cold and slithery under his feet. He then tried to do the impossible: run while still zipped up firmly in his sleeping bag. Twisting, turning, screaming, and dragging half the camp behind him, he reminded LW of a worm caught in a spider web. This was beyond funny. This was one for the ages, one to tell future generations.

The commotion awoke Henry, who joined in the laughter after he quickly checked his own sleeping bag. He could hear his cousin yelling unintelligibly back in the brush, and LW was rolling around, holding his side, and making squealing noises. Henry carefully checked his surroundings and, after a thorough inspection, began putting on his boots.

"LW, you better get up and run." Henry had heard the insulted party returning to the scene of the crime and could surmise by his language and volume that Billy had a pretty good idea that his bedfellow had not acted on its own. The ensuing fight was short-lived as Henry picked up his rod and tackle box and headed down to the river. LW and Billy soon tired of the fight and joined Henry on the bank.

The three boys spread out, and each chose his bait based on his perceived skills. LW went with crickets, in hope of filling a stringer with brim. Billy broke out a hoola popper in hopes of nailing a large mouth bass. His first cast brought him a tree limb, hanging the lure about three feet above the surface of the river.

"Now that was the best cast I've seen in years. Maybe you could take some time and show me how you do that."

"LW, you ought not to make fun of the guy who's about to set the record for biggest tree caught on an artificial bait," piped in Henry.

Billy took the rubbing and skillfully popped the lure back into the water only to have it get hooked again. This time, the water exploded as a five-pound bass ripped into the bait hanging just above the water line. "Well, the bait's free now," shot Billy in a tone that belied his arrogance. The other two boys were now watching the combatants as the fish did his level best to spit the offending item from its mouth, and Billy fought to keep it there. By the look on LW's face, one could not tell which side he was supporting, the bass or his cousin. Henry left room for no such debate as he openly supported the bass. Their screams and jibs made it sound like a wrestling match, and an even match at that. The bass exploded out of the water, walked on its tail, and then dove deep, heading for a sunken tree. Billy, knowing what his adversary's plan was, instinctively pulled back just enough to turn the fish and keep him from wrapping his line on the unseen underwater obstacle. Now both of the spectators saw the move and understood the skill involved in this and fell silent. LW stood in awe of the battle raging before his eyes. Neither player could gain an inch, yet neither would give an inch. It had, for the moment, deteriorated into a stalemate.

The bass had only two options: break the line or spit out the lure. The contest was drawing to its inevitable conclusion. The bass was tiring, and the line moved slowly towards the bank. About two feet from Billy, the bass made one final dive, gained speed, and soared out of the water. With its mouth agape, the fish gave a mighty flip of its head and the hoola popper came shooting up and hung around Billy's hat. The only evidence left of the victor was a small ripple that was slowly dissipating. Henry, who by this time was sitting beside his stunned cousin, was on the verge of uttering a nasty comment or two when he saw the hound dog expression written across Billy's face and thought better of it. LW had no such reserve and immediately begin ribbing has partner.

"Damn, Billy, if you were just going to let that big guy go, why make all the fuss and noise? Why didn't you just cut the line when he first got on?"

Billy quietly began to reel in his line and cast out again. Finding no fight in his cousin left LW feeling content, and off he went to harvest his brim. Unabashed by the glee he felt for the lost fish, LW slipped another worm on his hook and looked around for the best place to drop his line in. Spying a limb hanging out over the water, he begin to crawl along its length and lay suspended about two feet above the water. Balancing, he carefully lowered his line down and felt the first tug as reward for his labor. It did not take long for his stringer to begin to fill up, and he was beginning to feel quite proud of his accomplishment— so proud, in fact, that he decided it was time to go rub it in the face of his cousins. With that little thought of pleasure in his mind, he made his preparations for his retreat down the limb. That's when he noticed that he was not alone on the branch. Bill stood lightly on the far end, and he had Henry standing right beside him. Feeling a small twinge of alarm racing through him, LW asked in a gruff voice, "Ya'll come to see a real fisherman?" as he began to back up. Bill said nothing. He just began jumping up and down on the limb. Now panic set in at a fevered pitch.

"You stop that, Bill. I got a stringer full of fish, and I'll show you how to catch them once I get off this limb. We both can't be out here together, and Henry needs to get off, too." Ignoring the rambling, both boys jumped harder and harder.

LW began again, "We will need to clean them so we can eat lunch. I guess you will want to eat that bass you caught. Ha ha!"

The loud snap echoed up and down the river bottom. LW felt a sickening feeling in his stomach as the river rushed up to meet him. Still clinging to the limb, he managed to hold onto his worm bucket, rod, and stringer. Surrounded by darkness, he plunged toward the bottom nearly five feet below. Finally, he released his hold and kicked upward, only to be caught in the current, and tumbled down river. After what seemed an eternity to him, his feet found solid ground and he scrambled up the bank to safety. He could see his cousins still standing on the broken limb, laughing and taunting him. After he caught his breath, he began to let out a torrent of curses and tried to fight his way up the tree-infested bank. Forgotten and unnoticed, his hook lay twenty feet behind him, covered in worms. As he worked his way up the bank, cursing at the mud, the trees, and most of all his cousins, a twenty-pound catfish began nosing at the wad of worms.

He moved his rod to avoid the trees and continued his verbal assault. "And another thing, I think you both are lousy baseball ..." The catfish decided it liked the morsel laid in front of it and bit, and then bit harder. LW felt the tug, and somewhere deep down inside, he knew he was in trouble, but his mind was slow to compute this information. With the rod aimed behind him, he had no leverage. The catfish took the worms, but something was wrong. The food was being pulled in the opposite direction. The fish decided to pull hard, and in doing so, he set the hook himself.

LW never got out the words that were on the tip of his tongue, for when the catfish hit the bait, it sent him hurling back down the bank he had so recently traversed. LW was in a total state of confusion. One minute he was fighting his way to the top of the bank and now he was falling back in the river again.

Billy and Henry were also stunned. They were preparing to repel an attack, and then LW jumped backwards into the river. This act, though impressive, was so shocking and inconceivable that the boys just stared at one another. To make matters worse, LW had reemerged and seemed to be fighting an invisible opponent. Up to his neck in water, he was laughing and screaming at nothing. His cousins began to worry he had a head injury, when LW did something even stranger. He jumped deeper into the river. One moment he was there, and the next, he was gone.

LW had recovered from his initial shock and soon realized the culprit behind his undignified plunge back into the river. He found that the fish now had all the advantages. Besides almost drowning and receiving a slight concussion from the impact, he had only pieces of his fishing rod left. Fortunately, his rod had taken the brunt of the fall. It had snapped just above the handle, leaving him almost nothing but the reel. Quickly realizing he could not hold out long, he dove to find the rest of his rod dangling just below the surface. Once this was secured, he began to crawl up the bank again, this time backwards, with both hands holding on to the rod, the bait bucket and stringer lost in the struggle.

Almost as quickly as he had vanished, he reappeared and began to simultaneously scream and crawl up the bank backwards. This was too much. Both Henry and Billy ran down to help their cousin against the mysterious threat. By the time they reached him, both could see the broken rod and the deranged look in LW's eyes. The boys just stood there, transfixed, more amazed at the language that was continuously erupting from LW than from the creature on the other end of the rod. That catfish was beginning to tire and slowly made his final ascent to the surface.

Now that the fight seemed about over and the situation under control, LW began to look around for his lost items. His stringer was nowhere to be seen, but his bait bucket was hung up in some brush, half in and half out of the water.

Soon the fish broke water, and all three got their first look at what LW had been fighting. He was huge, at least three feet in length, with barbels extending out eight inches from his head. It truly looked like a monster from the deep. The catfish, now only a few feet away, finally got a break. LW had turned to smart off to Billy, and in so doing, he allowed his line to snag on a tree root lying at edge of the river. With one last defiant tug, the fish snapped the line just above the cork. The fish, now free, was slowly sinking back into the river, almost too exhausted to swim. LW turned with a scream of outrage and shock and then leaped back into the river for the third time that day. For the two cousins, this was simply too much to bear. They both began roaring. LW, who was now engrossed in hand-to-hand combat with the fish, was totally oblivious to the offending laughter.

After a few minutes of violent battle, the river fell silent as LW slowly pulled his vanquished foe up the bank. "Ha! That's the way you land a fish. No messing around, no fancy rod work, just plain old-fashioned muscle." The fish seemed about the same size as LW, who was slowly pushing it up the muddy bank. He was repeating the same action he was so doggedly pursuing before ending up in the river: trying to get up the bank.

Henry commented to Billy that LW was the luckiest guy he had ever heard of. Although he was utterly exhausted, LW's mouth was working at just the same speed as earlier, only this time, it was spewing praise for himself and heaping scorn on his cousins. As he reached the top of the bank, Billy took the fish, and Henry began helping LW up. Just as he took Henry's hand, LW remarked how much his cousins reminded him of a bunch of girls. With one heave, Henry sent him rolling back down into the river. For the fourth time that day, he landed in the water, and the frustration was turning into murderous rage.

Henry was eyeing his cousin, trying to gauge how long it would take him to reach the top again, deciding that with the well-worn path that marked LW's earlier climbs, it would not take long. Billy sat by the fish, totally ignoring the other two. He was meticulously trying to push a large stick through the mouth of the catfish. Henry was still watching LW, who seemed to be laughing—in madness or humor he could not yet tell.

"You starting to like that water or what?" Henry asked.

"Hell no. I found my stinger."

"Lucky SOB," Billy muttered, finally succeeding in installing the stick. Henry just stared in disgust, turned without uttering a word, and picked up one end of the stick.

The boys decided that with the black clouds in the distance and the mess of fish, they had better head home. Besides, neither Henry nor Billy felt like listening to LW, who had, by this time, managed to crawl up the bank and return to camp.

By the time the boys returned home, the weather had turned nasty. Lightning lit up the sky, and the wind started blowing hard enough to rock their car. They had cleaned the brim they had caught and divided it up between them, but the catfish remained untouched. While Billy drove, Henry sat and stared at the monster his cousin had somehow brought into their world. LW had not stopped adding to his laurels, not even to take a breath.

"I doubt there are many people alive who have seen a fish like this," LW stated with pride.

"I know there is going to be one less if you don't shut up," Bill said in a very threatening manner.

LW had been relentless in his praises and continued now unabated. "I mean, just think about it: my picture in the morning paper, holding up my trophy. I am going to be famous."

Billy felt himself getting nauseous. He had an almost overwhelming desire to brutally beat his cousin. The very thought brought him a sense of euphoria. At the last instant, he realized he had passed LW's house and slammed on the breaks.

"Well, Billy is in such shock over my fish he doesn't even know where he is." LW's voice bit hard into Billy, whose only thought was to get that braggart out of his car.

LW entered his house like a conquering hero, his trophy held out before him for all to see. His mother came out from the den to scold him for being out in the rain. One look at the creature her son was holding and all comprehensible language died in her throat. Instead, an ear-piercing scream became a prelude to a panicked and undignified retreat.

"Get that God-awful thing out off my house," she yelled.

This did nothing but add to LW's delight. His father was caught off guard as his wife came running by, swatting at him and yelling at LW.

"What the hell is wrong with you, Annie?" he demanded.

"That awful son of yours brought some kind of disgusting creature home with him," she replied.

LW Sr. got up in a fit of rage, only to trip on his footrest and fall flat on his face. Spitting and cursing, he rounded the corner, ready to take out his wrath on his unscrupulous son, who was, at this time, standing sheepishly, holding out his fish. Upon seeing the object of his wife's duress, LW Sr. stopped so quickly he almost fell again. Anger was slowly replaced by awe, which then gave way to pride.

"Well my gawd, that sure is a monster. How did you catch it?" LW Sr. asked. His son now had a captive audience and went into a five-minute tirade about how he had outsmarted the fish and his cousins, outfought them all, and did it all one handed. The father heard only parts of it as he moved off to get his camera. Besides, he knew better than anyone that he would never hear the real story.

About that time, his mother's voice echoed from her room. "Is that thing still in my house, because if it is, you two will be sleeping outside tonight."

"Dang it, woman. The boy has caught a record fish, and I would like to get a picture of it!"

LW Sr. was having his own difficulties. The camera was being elusive. He knew it was on the top shelf of the hall closet, but he just could not quite locate it. LW was tired of holding the fish up and finally stopped trying, allowing the fish to lower until half its body was resting on the carpet. His attention was now riveted on his father, stretching high into the closet. It was only a matter of time. The camera had finally been located, just beyond his reach. He needed only to stretch another fraction of an inch.

There was a loud bang, and LW Sr. felt the top shelf fall beneath his weight. LW had been eagerly awaiting this exact event, licking his lips in anticipation. LW Sr. felt his support suddenly disappear as the top shelf gave way, and he fell headfirst into the back wall, taking the middle shelf with him. The explosion of noise drew LW's mother from her hiding place. As she entered the living room, she was astounded to see her husband lying on the closet floor with what appeared to be the entire inventory of their hall closet piled on top of him.

On closer inspection, she saw a hole about the size of a man's head in the back wall, at approximately the same level that the top shelf should have been. The shock was so great that the only sounds she could manage were "Wha ... wha ... wha ..." This was all too much for LW, and he began to laugh uncontrollably. His mother, upon hearing his laughter, turned slowly and saw a big slimy fish lying on her new carpet. To LW's amazement, his mother quickly found her voice.

"Get out, you little urchin! I cannot believe that you would set that thing down on my carpet. Oooout!"

LW wisely retreated to a safer area. Though still laughing, he recognized the anger in his mother's eyes. So back out into the storm he went, dragging his trophy behind him.

LW Sr. had finally regained his feet and secured the camera. His wife, with her son now safely out of her reach, turned upon her husband and began to belittle him. Her husband, though standing, was still dazed from his fall and still in shock over the shelves' collapse, which he took as a direct affront upon himself. He was now apparently under attack from another direction. His wife had him fully in her sights and was holding none of her anger back.

"Now wait just a minute. I was just in an accident, and I could be hurt bad," he stated in a weak attempt.

"I will show you hurt bad. Now get out of my house!" she replied angrily.

He thought about pointing out the fact that the whole closet thing was just an accident, and it was his house, too. Then saw the same anger in her eyes and thought better of it. He soon followed his son's trail outside.

With most of her rage spent, LW's mother looked around numbly, like a survivor of some great tragedy. The speed with which her house had been befouled and destroyed was mind-boggling. She was torn between her desire to clean up the mess and her wish to exact her vengeance upon its authors. After a moment's hesitation, she decided to start on the carpet first. LW Sr. found his son in the garage, still holding his fish. His angry words died in his throat as he inspected his son's catch. Still holding his painfully acquired camera, he finally took his pictures. LW's chest puffed out more with each click of the camera. "We will get this in the paper," LW Sr. stated. The two then cleaned the fish and prepared it for a future meal.

LW had finally finished paying his penance with three days of hard labor. His mother was still unhappy about her carpet and swore that she could smell fish. She was, however, the only one who could detect this particular odor.

The first morning of freedom brought him inevitably to Bill's house. A fact that his cousin had not yet decided whether this was good or bad. But the moment he saw the item in LW's hand, he knew it was bad. LW proudly showed off his new prize: yesterday's paper. LW's beaming face smiled at him. He then added insult to injury by offering to autograph it for his cousin.

"What are you doing, Billy?"

"I am trying to figure out what I am going to do after school."

"School doesn't start for another two days. I'd say you have a little while to figure that out."

"I wasn't talking about after school next week. I am talking about after graduation," Bill replied.

"That's a long time away." LW was confused by this line of thought.

"It's a long time away for you, but I am three years older."

LW sat stunned, and for the first time, he realized the implications of their age difference. "So, do you have to go to work or something?" LW was becoming as forlorn as his cousin.

"Well, I got a letter from the army yesterday," Bill said absentmindedly.

"What? Why would they be writing you?" LW demanded, getting more confused by the minute.

"Because of the draft. I have been ordered to report for basic training the first week of July." Now LW was completely bewildered. His world had just been altered, really for the first time. An entity beyond his understanding had just reached down and tapped him on the shoulder. He and his cousins had big plans for the summer. How could the army do this? Why did they need his cousin? There were thousands of guys with nothing to do, so there was no reason to pick on Billy. Well that settled it. Billy would just have to skip his appointment. LW could think of a few things that they could do to make his cousin stay home. It didn't make any sense. His whole summer ruined, and for what?

"Why don't you just not go?" LW asked.

"Oh, yeah, just not show up so they can declare me AWOL and arrest me. That makes a lot of sense."

LW was appalled. "They could arrest you?"

Billy gave him a cold stare and decided that there was no hidden sarcasm in the question. "Yes, they can arrest you, stupid. That's what you call draft dodging."

LW's alarm was growing so fast that he completely missed that fact that his cousin had just called him stupid. The two boys just sat there, each with his own thoughts. Finally, LW got up and headed home. His father might be able to explain this a little better.

LW Sr. was bemused by his son's confusion over the draft issue. "But, Dad, how can the army just take someone for no reason? I mean, it's not like this person did something wrong." LW was not getting the answers that he wanted.

"Listen, son, after graduation from high school, every man is eligible for the draft. You see, our country has to defend itself, and it needs soldiers to do that."

"But, Dad, if everyone got drafted, there would not be any men left."

LW Sr. had to try hard not to laugh. "Son, you only serve for one year, and besides, at least one-third of all recruits are rejected."

"What do you mean, rejected?"

"Well, some men have health problems, like bad hearing or vision, so the army sends them home." LW was finally getting the answers that he was waiting for.

"So, if someone has something wrong with him, then he doesn't have to go to the army?"

"Yes, exactly." LW Sr. felt an odd buzz way back in his mind, like a little warning bell, but for the life of him, he could not determine how this line of questioning could lead to trouble.

"Thanks, Dad. I guess I will go see how Mom's doing."

LW Sr. thought the whole conversation was a little strange, but conversations with his son often were. Later, he went in to wash up for lunch, the morning's conversation long forgotten.

"What's for lunch?" he asked. His wife dropped a meatloaf sandwich in front of him and sat down with a smile.

"That son of yours ran off with his sandwich. I guess he wants to spend as much time with Billy as he can."

Her husband's reply was muffled. "Why would he need to spend time with Billy?"

"You should not talk with your mouth full. Because Billy got drafted. He reports for duty the first of next month." Her reply caused LW Sr. to choke on his sandwich. "You need to take smaller bites. I know your mother taught you better than that." Her husband barely acknowledged her comments.

Henry arrived in time to see LW chasing Billy around with a bat.

"This will only hurt for a second," LW yelled. Billy did not think that was true, but he was not going to find out.

"Hold still. I don't want to bash the wrong part. We need to break something big," LW said as he took a swipe at his cousin's legs.

Billy, seeing the arrival of a possible ally, turned and ran directly at Henry. Billy   arrived just as LW took another swing, and Henry had to chose which one he would avoid. He ducked beneath the incoming bat. Billy hit Henry full on, like a linebacker making a tackle. Both boys went rolling on the ground, with LW swinging away like Babe Ruth.

"Now hold up there, Lawrence. What's this all about?" Henry inquired.

"Billy's been drafted, and the only way he can stay home is if he has something wrong with him." Henry saw the logic in LW's thought process.

"Don't tell me that you agree with this homicidal maniac," Billy pleaded.

"No, I don't agree with his methods, but he does have a point."

LW stood listening to the debate. He could not decide if he had an ally or an enemy. He tightened his grip on his bat just in case Henry chose to side with Billy.

"He's never had a valid point in his whole life, and you know it," Billy said darkly.

"Look, the fact is, unless you've got something wrong with your body, you're in the army." Henry was staring thoughtfully at Billy.

"All I was trying to do was help you, and you know it," LW stated.

"Bull. You just want a hunting pard for the summer. I doubt my well-being ever crossed your mind. All you ever think about is yourself."

The accusation in his voice made Henry feel bad. LW, on the other hand, looked like he was about to take another shot at his cousin.

"You don't know what you're talking about. I had only concern for you."

Billy rolled his eyes. "Did it ever occur to that I might want to join the army?"

Henry was shocked. It had never occurred to either of the other two that Billy might actually want to go.

"I am sorry, Billy. I had no idea that you felt that way," Henry said.

"That's my point. Neither of you took the time to ask me."

"Okay, Bill, if that's how you feel, I'll accept it, and I am sorry."

Billy stared at Henry and felt his apology was genuine. Both boys came to a quiet understanding and then looked over at the third member of their threesome.

"How about you, LW? Can you accept my decision?" Billy inquired.

LW stood staring at the two. "Hell no. You are just confused, that's all. I think you will thank me for getting you out of the army."

Billy had had enough, but before he could say a word, Henry punched LW in the nose and sent him flying.

"I'll tell you who's confused, and that's you. You're not thinking of Billy. You are thinking of yourself. Billy wants to go, and that's final. Now either you can accept that and let him go, or you can fight the both of us right now," Henry screamed at him.

Billy stood in shocked amazement at his defender. He looked down at LW, waiting for the counter attack, but LW just sat there holding his nose and staring back at Henry. Henry, for his part, was beyond caring. If LW wanted a fight, he had one coming. Finally, LW stood up and looked back and forth between the two boys.

"Well, fine, if you feel that strongly about it, go on, but don't expect me to cry at your funeral when you get shot in some war." Henry began to breathe a little easier. LW was hell on wheels in a fight.

Billy was even more stunned by this turn of events. Never in a million years would he have thought that he would see LW get knocked down and not come up fighting. Maybe Henry had knocked some sense into him.

LW started walking back to his house, leaving a blood trail behind, when his father drove up. Henry thought that he might be in trouble when he saw the worried look on his uncle's face. LW Sr. looked from his son's bleeding nose to the two cousins and then to the now disregarded bat.

"What happened?" he asked.

Henry started to reply when he was interrupted by LW. "I was being hardheaded, but I have seen the error of my ways."

Billy found this to be funny, and soon all three boys were laughing. LW Sr. smiled a knowing smile and sighed in relief. Whatever mischief his son was up to seemed to have been averted. LW got into his father's car and waved good-bye to his cousins.

"Well, it looks like Billy's going to go through with it."

His father looked confused. "Was there ever any doubt?"

LW was looking out the window. "For a minute or two."

LW, Billy, and Henry were sitting on the railroad bridge, throwing fire crackers into the Trinity River. School was out for the summer, and Billy was leaving the next day. The boys were unusually quiet, each absorbed in his own thoughts. LW felt miserable. Billy was leaving, and there was no way to stop it. He had resolved himself to his fate. Henry cleared his throat and said, "I joined the army today." The statement hung in the air with no response from his cousins.

Henry felt a need to explain. "I figured it's only a matter of time before I receive my notice, so I thought they would treat me better if I were a volunteer." Again, nothing but silence. LW felt like he'd been kicked in the stomach. Now he was losing both his cousins, his best friends. It was simply too much. LW got up and started walking off. This was the saddest day in his young life.

Henry watched him go and then turned to Billy. "What the hell was that all about? You would think he would say something—I mean yell or cuss or something."

Billy was watching LW walk away. "Now you're doing to him exactly what I did."

Henry stared at his cousin. "What are you talking about?"

Billy looked sad. "Think about Lawrence for a moment. We have all grown up together, we go on vacation together, we are family, and we are best friends. It was hard enough for him to let me go; now he is losing both of us. He has a year of school left, and for the first time in his life, it will be without us."

Henry slowly turned this over in his mind and began to understand what LW must be feeling.

"So where and when do you have to report?" Bill asked.

"I report in two weeks, somewhere down in Mississippi."

Bill got up. "Well, that's got to be better than me. I am training in California."

Henry chuckled. "Yeah, right. Who would want to train on the beach?"

Billy smiled. "Maybe I'll get a tan and drink some fancy concoctions with little umbrellas." Both boys enjoyed a good laugh and finished off the last of their firecrackers.

"I guess I'll head on home. See you at the train tomorrow," Henry said, waving good-bye. Billy stayed around for a while throwing rocks and contemplating the future.

Chapter Three

The train was running on time for once. Billy was there with his parents. Henry had ridden with him, and Bill's girlfriend had come along for the ride. Well, to be correct, Katy was now his fiancée, though no one other than their parents knew that. Just as the train pulled up, so did LW and his father. Billy thought that he was going to cry as he watched his red-eyed younger cousin walk up to him.

LW had been unable to sleep. He had visions of car wrecks, falls, and fights. But his cousins seemed to have made it to the train station in one piece. His parents, knowing the sadness he was feeling, had left him alone for most of the night. LW had sat out on the front porch for three hours, until his father had come out and sat down beside him.

"Son, I can only imagine what you must be going through, but it's only for one year, and they will be back before you know it."

LW sighed. "I know it, and besides, it's not like there is a war going on." His father did not answer, but inside he wasn't sure about his son's view on a peaceful year.

Father and son spent a half hour sitting quietly together before LW Sr. got up to go to bed. "Shut the screen door when you come in. The bugs are bad out here."

LW was happy that his father had joined him, but he was also glad when his father decided to go to bed. LW finally came into the house at about two in the morning.

Now, as he walked up to Billy, he felt his stomach turning. Though grief-stricken, he was determined not to show it.

"So you decided to show up," Billy said. LW felt like crying but instead forced out an acceptable reply.

"I figured you would cry like a girl if I didn't."

Henry smiled and turned to Billy. "You know, it's still not too late. You could still break something."

Billy laughed. LW perked up for a moment. His father had looked strangely at him when he loaded his bat in the car. "Just in case," he stated weakly. He saw that his cousins were only making a joke, and his spirits fell again. The train whistle blew, and the boys exchanged quick handshakes as Billy ran to jump on the train.

"Bye. When I get back, I will show you both how to shoot." LW stood waving until the train was far out of sight. Soon, the only sound was the crying of Billy's mother and girlfriend.

"Hey, LW, do want to go get a root beer?" asked Henry.

"I guess so. There ain't much else to do." With that, the boys headed downtown. LW Sr. thought about offering them a ride and then decided that they needed time together.

Henry and LW stopped by the Trinity and began throwing rocks at the ducks and frogs. Both boys were depressed, and neither talked. LW got up and walked down toward the river. He was lost in his own thoughts. If he felt this bad without Billy, how would he feel with both Henry and Billy gone? Henry looked up to see LW balancing on a bridge beam just a few feet above the waterline. He got up and walked over to his young cousin and then pushed him into the river. LW surfaced to find Henry laughing, and after a moment, he joined in the laughter. The heartbreak over Billy began to recede. Henry took off his shirt and jumped in. The boys splashed around and wrestled with each other. After a while, they made their way up the bank and headed for that root beer.

Conley's Five and Dime was almost deserted when they made their way to their seats. The building was one of the oldest structures in downtown that was still in use. It's hard wood floors were stained and well worn. A large counter stood at one side, and four rows of shelves ran the length of the other. It did not take much imagination to see how the layout still mirrored its humble beginnings as a frontier saloon. Mr. Conley saw the cousins about twice a week. This was the first time he had ever seen two just of them. As he poured their drinks, he decided to inquire as to the whereabouts of the third amigo.

"So what did you boys do with Billy?" Neither boy seemed to hear his question, so Mr. Conley repeated it with a note of concern in his voice.

Henry looked up and said, "The army got him."

Mr. Conley almost burst out laughing. The sadness in the two boys prevented that.

"Well, I am glad to hear it." LW wanted to know why he was glad, but before he could ask, Mr. Conley continued. "I can remember my army days. We spent the first six weeks working out and learning how to be soldiers. There were near a hundred of us living in one barrack. Each of us had our own bunk and trunk. Every morning, we would report for some kind of special training. One day would be rifle practice or maybe pistol practice. And then there was my favorite, grenade practice. We would lob those things as far as we could. Blew up everything we could find. Got to shoot artillery and mortars, though those kinda hurt your ears. And the food, now it wasn't your mamma's cooking, mind ya, but there was lots of it. And none of it cost us a dime; the army paid for all of it. Then there were the weekend passes; the army would give you your two weeks pay and send you into a town just filled with women. And of course, no one cared about your age. You could drink all the beer you wanted."

LW could not believe his ears. This sounded a lot like camp—a camp that let you blow things up and gave you money to do it.

"You mean that the army pays you? And they let you blow things up?" LW asked. Henry was staring at Mr. Conley with his mouth wide open. Mr. Conley was staring off into the distance, lost in his memories. LW was starting to get angry. Here he was, feeling sorry for Billy, and he was off for the time of his life. Not only was Billy going to have a blast, he was going to be paid for it.

"I should have known. Billy lied to us. Here we are feeling sorry for him, and he is probably laughing his head off right now. I ought to find him and beat his head in," LW said with disgust.

Henry looked at his cousin and stated the obvious. "You weren't feeling sorry for him, and he didn't know how much fun the army was."

"How do you know he didn't know?" asked LW.

"Because we didn't know, so how could he?"

LW did not hesitate. "He got a letter and talked with the army. You think they didn't tell him? Why wouldn't they? I mean, no wonder he looked like he was acting this morning at the train. He acted all sad, and the whole time he couldn't wait to get out of here."

"LW, I got a letter, and it didn't say anything about it," Henry said angrily.

"You got a letter, but you haven't talked with them yet. I'll bet they don't say anything until right before you leave."

"That doesn't make any sense. Why wouldn't they tell you?"

"Think about it. They only let so many guys in there a year. They pick the ones that they want and tell them not to talk about it. It's like a club. You don't want everyone to know how fun your club is or everyone would want to join."

The more he thought about it, the madder LW was getting. How like Billy it was to keep something so great a secret. It was always like that. He and Henry got to do all the fun stuff first, and later they would share it with their younger cousin. It was always like that, a plot to keep him out of their fun, Billy and Henry...

Henry didn't like the way his cousin was looking at him. He had seen that look before. "LW, I just don't think that Billy would do that to us."

"You mean do that to you. No, he wouldn't."

"I don't know what you mean, but I am sure that Billy would not do that to you, either," Henry said.

"So you were in on it from the beginning. I should have known. Well, the games up, pard. Cuz now I know, and I am going to tell everyone. Let's see how your little club likes that," LW said with a wolfish grin. LW threw a dime down to pay for his drink and headed out the door.

Henry was concerned. What if LW was right? It was an unbelievable occurrence, but maybe this once he was correct. But if the army was that fun, why didn't his uncle tell him it was? He could hear LW's answer to that question: it's all about the code. Keep it a secret, and only certain people would ever know. It was probably one of those secrets that are sworn in blood. You probably got kicked out if you told. His thoughts returned to LW. *Oh no, what if LW tells? They might not take me.* With this thought in his head, Henry dropped his dime and headed for the door. It was only after the door closed that Mr. Conley realized that he had lost his audience and stopped talking.

Henry stared up and down First Street. His cousin wasn't anywhere to be seen. That was good, Henry thought. If LW headed straight home, maybe, just maybe, he wouldn't see anyone and couldn't open his big mouth. As Henry headed toward the bridge, he saw a group of boys coming around the corner, talking excitedly to each other. Henry continued toward the river at a fast walk when the leader of the group saw him.

"Hey, Henry, wait up for a minute." Henry slowed but didn't stop

"What do you want?" he asked.

"Is it true?"

"Is what true?" Henry asked. He was holding his breath now, waiting for the question he feared would be asked.

"Is the army like a big camp? Is it true they let you blow things up and drink all the beer you want, and that they pay you to do it?"

Henry thought that he was going to be sick. "You guys know better than to listen to him. He's just pulling your leg. Now which way did LW go?"

"How would we know? We haven't seen him."

"What? Then who told you about the army?"

"Harold did."

Henry started off toward the bridge, this time at a jog. He spied Harold talking to someone in a car.

"Harold, have you seen LW?" The people in the car drove off.

"Yes, I saw him right after he told me about your little club."

"First of all, he is lying about that. Now which way did he go?"

"He told me you would deny it. I can't believe that you two wouldn't tell us about it."

"I didn't tell you because it's not true. Now stop telling people."

"He said you'd say that, and he told me I should tell ten people and tell them to tell ten people. Secret's out; now everyone will know."

Henry took off toward LW's house at a dead run. As he turned on to Riverside, he saw another group of boys, and he crossed the street in an effort to avoid them. Their voices carried well. "Henry, is it true?" He ran faster. By the time he reached LW's house, he was completely out of breath. He sat down on the porch and heard his uncle's car come out from behind the house and turn into the street. He was too late. He saw the face in the passenger's side looking back at him. LW was still smiling as he watched his cousin struggle to get up.

Henry heard the door open, and his uncle came out. "Hello, Henry. You just missed LW."

Henry hated to ask, but he had to know. "Where did he go?"

"His mother just took him down to the baseball fields. He was in an awful hurry."

Henry lay in bed that night, plotting ways to get back at LW. His cousin was like smallpox, spreading uncontrollably. Henry could almost hear the angry voices from the army: "We had a good thing going until we decided to let you in, Henry." He tossed and turned most of the night until sleep finally released him.

That next day, the army recruiter was ecstatic. He had already made his recruiting quota for the next four months. Boys were lining up around the block. He thought it must be that war in Europe. The pride he took in watching these boys joining up to do their patriotic duty made his chest swell.

LW had just completed his tale of army life to his father. The tale had grown to such magnificent proportions that it seemed stupid for a man not to join. His father was now laughing uncontrollably, tears began running down his cheeks.

"Where did you get this notion? I mean, did you actually talk to a recruiter or something?" LW did not know how to take his reaction. He had thought his father would be amazed at the information.

"Dad, this is true. It's like camp, but they pay you. They even give you clothes and drive you wherever you need to go." This made his dad laugh even harder.

LW's mother was growing concerned. It was funny, but if LW truly believed this nonsense, he might enlist. She decided that her husband was unfit at the present time to adequately explain the situation. "Son, the army is not a club. It's not fun and it's hard work. They make you get up before sunup every day and run for miles. You have to do what they tell you. The food is lousy, and you could even get sent to war. Yes, they pay you, but it's little or nothing. If they need a ditch dug, you dig it. They own you and are free to do with you what they want to. You cannot quit or leave unless they tell you that you can."

LW was stunned. This could not be true. "Mr. Conley said that his days in the army were the happiest of his life."

His father had begun to regain some of his composure. "Son, old men look back at the glory days of their youth through rose-colored glasses. What I mean is that the older you get, the better the past seems. If you talk to older people, they will always say the times they grew up in were better than the present. The fact is, the best time to be alive is now, whenever now is. If you could go back to when Mr. Conley was in the army, he would probably tell you that it was the worst thing on earth. The next time you see Mr. Conley, why don't you ask him why he is not still in the army."

This last part caught LW by surprise. Why wasn't Mr. Conley still in the army? Maybe you had to leave after a while, but if so, why would you keep it a secret? Maybe his parents were right. His father patted him on the back and walked out, laughing. His mother watched him for a second and then seemed satisfied and went back to the kitchen. LW headed for his tire swing to contemplate everything he had been told. He, like his cousin, tossed and turned all night long.

The following morning, Henry went in search of his cousin. He went to LW's house only to be directed down to the creek by his aunt.

"He's probably down there fishing. Henry, you be careful in the army. Just do what you're told and come back." His aunt had a troubled look in her eyes. Henry told her he would and then set off, looking for his elusive pard.

LW had been sitting by the creek for an hour. When Henry arrived, LW took no notice of him.

"What are you doing, LW?"

LW took his time answering. "Just thinking about Bill. Wondering how he's doing and if he is terribly lonely."

"I guess you gave up the idea of army life being all fun and games."

"Why? Did my dad tell you about it, too?"

"No. My father and I talked about it this morning. I didn't know it, but he was in the war," Henry replied.

LW perked up at this. "What war?"

"The Great War. He was an artillery man. He told me that there was nothing fun about it. He said it was a chore that young men had to do and it was hard. Said I was to do it and get out."

"Did you ask him what it was like? The war, I mean."

"He said it was hell on earth. People dying and screaming, poison gas everywhere. Said the food was half rotted and all the water was tainted. They had to sleep in the mud and did not have decent clothes." Both boys contemplated this for a minute and then decided to go look for crawfish.

The scene that was played out for Billy's departure was repeated for Henry. This time, LW got there earlier and tried to put a cheerful spin on the situation.

"Henry, I want you to have fun at camp. Don't drink too much beer." Both boys smiled at this.

"I'll see ya in a year," Henry said as he jumped onto the train.

LW stood by, watching the train pull out and thinking that his heart was going to break. His father put his arm around him, and they walked back to the car. His mother sat in the front seat with tears running down her face. She looked over at her husband, and they both shared the same thought: the next family member that they would see off would be their own son. He sat in the back of the car, oblivious to the concerns shared by his parents. His father took that moment to inform LW that they had decided to take a family trip to Yellow Stone National Park. This brought a surprised yelp from the back seat. LW Sr. informed the family that they would be leaving at sunup the following day.

The car was packed, and by eight the next morning, they were on their way. LW was brimming with excitement. He was overwhelmed by the endless possibilities. However, their first adventure was the wrong turn his father took just north of Wichita Falls. It took almost an hour before his parents realized their mistake. After much arguing and finger-pointing, they decided to stop for lunch. As LW wandered around the field they had decided picnic in, his parents were engrossed in a discussion of his future. LW Sr. looked at his wife and said, "You sure are beautiful." Even though he told her that at least twice a week, she never got tired of hearing it.

"You hush. What do you think the chances are that LW will be drafted?" she replied.

"I think the odds are pretty good. He is healthy and very intelligent."

"What can we do about it?" she inquired.

"Nothing. There's nothing we can do."

"He's just a little boy, too little to be going off to join the army."

LW Sr. put his arm around the girl he loved with all his heart. "He may be too little right now, but in a year, he will be a man."

LW's mother slid closer to her husband. "That's a year from now. Let's not mention it again until then." The warmth of her body and the love in her eyes killed any further comments from him.

LW could not believe the enormous distance they had traveled. Three days on the road and the country seemed to keep going on forever. Rolling plains gave way to forest-covered hills. Deer fed along the road, and herds of elk roamed the hillsides. Even such awesome distractions got old as the miles passed slowly by. His father had announced their arrival about five minutes before they saw the ranger station. The station had a restaurant and museum. It looked like a giant log cabin. A twelve-foot pine door was framed by two large lanterns. LW headed straight for the museum. The stuffed animals were fascinating, especially the grizzly bear. LW was amazed at the size of the beast. It was taller than his father, and they said it weighed one thousand pounds.

"Do you think we will get to see one of these alive?" His father was astounded. He had heard they were big, but this was incredible. The claws must have been six inches long. His mother was looking at the fur coats and missed the subject of the conversation.

"Yes, dear, you will probably see lots of them, probably close enough to touch 'em."

LW's eyes became as big as fifty-cent pieces. "Close enough … to touch them."

"That's right," she replied as she picked up another fur coat.

Who in their right mind would want to get close to one of these things. It dawned on LW that he would be sleeping in a tent. If these monsters were everywhere like his mother said, then that meant they would be just outside his tent. His father happened to be thinking the same thing. Both of them were staring at his mother when she glanced up from her shopping.

"What's wrong with you two? You look like you have seen a ghost."

LW thought a ghost might be a whole lot easier to deal with.

"Why would you tell your son that he would get close enough to touch a grizzly bear?"

"What grizzly bear? What on earth are you talking about?" She was bewildered. Somehow she had been involved in a conversation that she didn't remember having. And then she saw the bear. "My goodness, that's a big animal." She realized at that point what she had done. "I am sorry, LW. I wasn't paying attention to what you were asking. I am sure we won't see any animals like this." She then hurried off to find the park ranger.

Father and son stood staring into the eyes of the monster. LW finally remarked, "I do believe those claws could rip right through a tent." If he was expecting some sort of reassurance of safety from his father, he was disappointed.

"You bet they could. With the size of this thing, he could tear apart the tent by just running into it. Probably would not even slow down." It got quiet while the men contemplated these words.

"Dad, do you have a gun?"

"Yes, I do, but don't tell anyone. Especially your mother. They might make me leave it here at the station." LW had no intention of betraying that gun. He needed it for survival. When his mother returned, it was with the park ranger in tow.

"The ranger assures me that we will not see one of these bears. Isn't that right?"

The ranger looked a little taken aback by this statement. "Like I was telling your mother, these bears are extremely rare. Most of what you will see are black bears."

LW's mother took over from there. "Did you hear that? These bears are extinct." Now all three men stared at her.

The ranger tried to defend himself. "Now that's not quite ..."

She had heard enough and began pushing her family out the door. LW managed to get a hold of the rules and safety tips pamphlet as he was ushered outside. The paragraph on bear safety caught his eye. It stated that contrary to his mother's remarks, grizzlies were alive and well in Yellow Stone. He began reading the rules out loud. "Rule one: if you see a bear, do not approach it. Rule two: bears are attracted by the smell of food, so keep ice chests out of tents and dispose of trash as far away from the camping area as possible."

His mother had heard enough about bears. "LW, stop reading and give me that pamphlet." He reluctantly handed over his life line.

Once they reached the camping area, LW and his father began to pitch the tent while his mother prepared breakfast. Just as they completed their set up, they smelled delicious bacon frying in the pan. Soon, eggs began to sizzle, adding their aroma to the smorgasbord already alive in the air. His father headed over to the fire. "Boy, that sure smells good." LW felt his own stomach start to growl. They sat back and began enjoying the scenery.

"That food sure smells good. It's amazing how clear the air is. I'll bet you can smell that food a mile away," said LW Sr.

LW agreed with his father, and both realized that they weren't the only ones who could smell the food. After they were through eating, his mother told them to carry away the trash. However, LW and his dad knew that with the smell of food in the air, anyone carrying away the trash might as well have a bull's-eye on his back.

LW Sr. looked over at his son and said, "You heard your mother. Take that trash and throw it away."

LW was stunned. They were sending him out as bait.

His father went over to the bags and started going through the fishing gear.

"Don't forget to take it far from camp, and don't linger," his mother said.

LW looked from one parent to the other; neither met his gaze. And so, like a condemned man, he began his slow walk out into certain death. His father never looked up as LW walked out into the valley all alone. He could hear bears sneaking up from every direction and saw a bear behind every fallen tree. When he was about fifty yards from the tent, he turned and made sure he could still see his parents. Just then, he heard a loud snap from behind him, and the trash hit the ground. LW was off like a shot back to camp. The cause of this noise went undiscovered as LW took flight. The raccoon that had been awoken by the smell of food now came out of its tree and began poking around the discarded trash.

LW found his mother lying in a hammock, reading a book. His treacherous father was nowhere to be seen. He took some time to look over their surroundings. They had made camp in a valley surrounded by low mountains. A clear stream flowed through the middle of the valley, about twenty feet from camp. Cursing from that direction gave an indication of the whereabouts of his father. LW soon joined him in the prettiest little creek he had ever seen. He picked up the extra rod his father had set out for him. His fishing rod was unlike any LW had ever beheld. A fly rod is what his father called it. LW was unimpressed. The fish must be pint-size if you could catch them on this thing.

LW was having a hard time throwing out his line. The lure, or fly as it was called, was so light, it refused to go more than a few feet across the water. He looked over at his father, who did not seem to be having much luck either, and asked, "Are you sure this is really how you do it?" He then felt a tug and looked over at his fly only to see a fish dangling in the air. He was astounded. How in the world had that happened?

"I got one! Look, Dad, I got one," he screamed.

"Way to go, son. Now drop him in the basket." LW did as he was told and then started the painful-looking dance of throwing out his line all over again. His line touched the water twice, and then, on the third time, another fish appeared on his hook.

"Hey, I got another one! Wow this is great."

LW Sr. was getting irritated. His line landed on everything except the water. His son, on the other hand, was catching fish left and right. He whipped his line back and forth and finally saw it touch the water. He felt a tug on his line, and when he lifted it up, there was a four-inch trout hanging on to his fly. It took all of five seconds for LW to see his father's trophy.

"I didn't know we were fishing with minnows."

His father bit his lip and said, "You're sure being cocky for someone who's fishing with a borrowed rod."

LW started laughing and moved farther upstream. It took the fishermen about three hours to fill their basket with fish. By the time they went to clean them, the bear issue had long been forgotten. LW had to admit it: this was the most incredible country he had ever seen.

That night, they sat around the campfire, enjoying their fresh trout. LW listened to his mother reading some of her book out loud. The stars were out in full, and the moon had just crested the mountain, when a much-feared guest made his long-awaited appearance. LW Sr. had just reached out to put a log on their small fire when he looked up into the face of a massive black bear. He was in complete shock. The bear had appeared so suddenly that his mind raced to grasp the situation. He remained frozen in the act of dropping the log onto the fire. His hand was forgotten on the now burning log. The spell was broken when the fire reached his fingers.

LW was chewing on a twig, contemplating the full moon. He was satisfied in every way. The only concern he had was his now too-tight belt. He relieved this problem and sighed contentedly. The perfect evening was shattered by his father's yelp of pain. LW laughed as his dad ran into their tent, holding his hand and yelling. His laughter was interrupted by a small voice in his head. Did his dad yell something about a bear? LW stared toward the darkness on the other side of the campfire. As his eyes adjusted, he could just make out the outline of the bear. LW yelled out and headed for the tent. He crashed into his father, who was coming out with his gun. Both men went tumbling in a heap. His mother had watched all that had transpired and now turned her attention to the unwanted guest. She had been enjoying a peaceful evening with her family; the silence they shared had been like ointment to her soul. How dare this bear ruin such a perfect moment!

The bear could not make out the figures moving beyond the light. His only thought was to find the source of that delicious smell. His nose had led him here, and now that nose was in pain. He let out an earth-shattering roar and fled back into night. LW and his father had recovered in time to see the cause of the bear's pain. His mother had reacted violently to the rude interruption. She had jumped up and retrieved a burning log from the fire. She then proceeded to hit the bear square in the noise with it. She stood listening to the wounded bear's retreat and then dropped the log back into the fire and sat down in her chair. She had made the entire attack in utter silence. Without a word, she picked up her book and went back to reading. Both men, feeling quit foolish, returned to the fire and sat contemplating the tiny woman they both loved so much. After a few minutes, LW's mother spoke up.

"LW, go get the first aid kit from the tent. And why did you bring a gun on this trip without telling me?" His father stammered for an answer. Both of her men spent the rest of that night in an embarrassed silence.

The next five days were spent hiking, fishing, and horsing around. There were few other bear encounters and many more fish caught. By the end of the trip, both men were expert fly fishermen. As they drove home, all three of them felt a sense of sadness and remorse. For the remainder of their lives, this trip would be held as the most precious time they had ever spent together. It is these moments that bind our dreams and memories of ages and people long gone.

*****

When LW returned from his vacation, he spent his first day back at the creek, swimming. On his way home, he came across Doris walking her dog. She looked radiant. Her hair was done up in pigtails. To his surprise, she smiled and stopped to talk to him.

"Hello, LW. Where have you been?"

"My family went on vacation to Yellow Stone Park."

"Really? What was it like?" she inquired.

"It was pretty nice, I guess. We saw lots of animals," he replied.

"Have you heard from either of your cousins?"

"Not yet, but I am sure they're doing all right. So how's Harold?" he asked. This question was of the greatest importance to him though he did not show it.

"I don't know, and I don't care," she replied.

LW felt like doing cartwheels. "Ya'll didn't break up, did you?" he asked hopefully.

"Yes, we did, although we're still friends. I don't think I will ever date a boy who's in the army again."

Now LW was confused. "Harold's in the army? I had no idea that he got drafted."

"He didn't. All he could talk about was how much fun it was going to be and how he had heard that it was a secret club. Then he went and signed up for three years. Can you believe it? Three years. And the army is some kinda club! How dumb can you be? I mean, really, where would he even come up with an idea like that?"

"I don't know. It sounds really dumb to me, too," LW stuttered.

She blushed a little. "Would you like to walk me home?"

"You bet. I mean, that would be great." LW walked her to her house and turned to leave. "Well, I guess this is it."

"I guess so," she replied.

LW decided to take a chance. "Do you think, maybe … you might want to get a hamburger or something?"

She smiled. "That would be nice."

LW couldn't believe his ears. "Well, okay, when do you want to do it?"

"How about you pick me up at, say, five thirty?"

He was floored. He never dreamed that she would want to go out with him, let alone tonight.

She looked a little concerned. "If five thirty isn't good, we could do it some other time."

"No, five thirty is great. I'll see you then."

He felt like he was walking on air as headed home. This was so completely unexpected. He had never been on a date. He'd never even been out with a group that included girls.

When he got home, he found his dad fighting with his lawn mower in the backyard. It looked to LW like the lawn mower was winning.

His father looked up and noticed the perplexed look on his son's face. "It's flooded, I think. What's eating you?"

LW decided to just come out with it. "I met this girl on the way home. She goes to my school, and she asked me to walk her to her house. So I did, and then I asked her to go eat a hamburger with me, and she said yes. Now I don't know what to do."

LW Sr. smiled despite himself. His little boy was becoming a man. He felt pride swelling up inside him. "Does this girl have a name?"

"Yes."

"Well, what is it."

LW was lost in his own thoughts. "What is what?"

"Her name," his father replied.

"Oh, it's Doris."

"Okay, that's a start. What you're going to do is go take a shower and start getting ready. Then I will take you over there to pick her up and meet her parents."

The thought that his dad would be going with him gave him a sense of relief.

When his mother asked why he was showering so early, the answer brought tears to her eyes. She became so smothering that LW grew concerned.

His father stood at the door, smiling at the thought of how his son had grown. "Leave the boy alone. He's gonna be late," his father said.

"Okay, just let me hold him for a second," his mother replied tearfully.

LW finally escaped her clutches and began dressing. When he came out of his room, his mother was nowhere to be seen. His father had the car keys in his hand and headed out the door. LW saw his mother standing at her bedroom window, and he waved good-bye.

Meeting Doris's father was much easier than LW thought it would be. His father seemed to know him, and the two started talking about the war in Europe. LW had been forgotten, and this was just fine with him. Doris's mother was a totally different matter all together. From the moment she walked out onto the porch, she glared at LW. As her husband introduced her to LW Sr., a quick smile crossed her lips. LW got a distinct feeling that he had just witnessed a rare occurrence. She then turned her glare back upon LW. She looked him up and down and then said, without blinking, "You have her back by seven o'clock and not a minute later."

"Yes, m-ma'am," LW stuttered. He was desperate to escape, when Doris finally made her appearance. Looking in her eyes gave him the confidence that he was so utterly lacking.

His father broke the silence by remarking on how beautiful she was. He then turned and shook hands with her parents and ushered the silent young couple towards the car. He threw a promise over his shoulder as he left. "Seven o'clock sharp."

LW was relieved to finally be back in the car, but now felt extremely shy. Once again, his father came to the rescue by asking Doris what her parents did for a living. During the rest of the drive, LW kept a dignified silence. He was afraid to open his mouth. His father had no such problems, easily slipping in and out of subjects and otherwise keeping the tension in the car at a tolerable level. Once inside the diner, LW felt naked and alone. Luckily, his father had given him some money before leaving. This was a good thing, because he had not thought of that and was penniless. His father had rescued him again.

He sat at the table and stared down at the menu, unable to master his shyness. After they ordered, Doris broke the silence. "Your father is very nice."

LW wished he could say the same thing. "Your parents weren't so bad, either," he replied.

She then said, "You look very nice."

"Thanks. So do you." He was glaring at some boys from his class, who thought his situation funny. Doris did not seem to notice the snickers from the corner. She went on to ask about his vacation. From there, the conversation became easier for him. Their food arrived, and the evening went off with out a hitch. By six thirty, his father pulled up outside, and LW was now head over heels in love. The ride home was over way too quickly. They were discussing world events, and LW had just stated that he did not believe that the Japanese would cause them any problems. After all, what possible reason could they have for wanting war with the United States?

They pulled into her driveway at six fifty. LW got out and opened her door and then walked her to her front porch.

"I had a great time," she said.

"So did I. Do you think I could come by tomorrow?"

"If you want to," she said shyly.

"Heck, yeah. Maybe we could go fishing sometime." She laughed and told him she would see him later. As she opened the door, the clock on the wall said six fifty-nine. LW stood looking at the closed door for a minute before turning and walking back to the car. He could not miss Doris's mother staring at him through the kitchen window. He waved, and she looked away without answering him.

Chapter Four

LW Sr. started up right where they left off. "I think maybe the war is getting closer to us."

"Dad, I just can't see the Japs wanting war with us."

"It may not be about wanting it; it might happen due to an accident."

"I don't think so. They're like on the other side of the world. They got no reason to fight us." Both men sat contemplating the worrisome prospect of a storm rising from a virtually unknown potential adversary. And neither could come up with a plausible scenario that could lead to war.

The Imperial Japanese council had to agree. Things were going extremely well. The entire southern coast of China was in their hands. Korea had fallen easily, as had most of South East Asia. Their navy, with its vaunted carriers, had lived up to their boasts, sweeping the seas clean of enemy ships. Tojo, the council's commander and the true power in Japan, had listened to the reports without comment. They had not mentioned the one issue that mattered most. Everyone in the room had absolutely no doubt as to the eventual and complete certainty of Japan's victory, save two men: Tojo and the commander of his navy. Out of all the men in the room, Tojo knew that he could trust the commander's opinion the most. He asked a question directed at no one. "Is it now true that our armies are unbeatable?" A resounding yes echoed through the chamber. Keeping his eyes locked on his admiral's eyes, he asked, "Is it now true that our navies are unstoppable?" Again, the room reverberated with an absolute yes. Still he stared at the man who sat quietly, not answering his questions. "Admiral Yammamotto, do you not share our enthusiasm? If there are reasons to doubt, please speak up."

All eyes now turned to the legendary admiral. He slowly stood up and walked over to a map. "It is true that our forces have made impressive gains. In China, we have taken much land and many cities. We have defeated their armies in battle after battle." Everyone nodded in agreement. "But we have taken less than half the country. Korea has fallen, and yet the Soviet Union lies just beyond the next mountain. We wiped the French out of Vietnam, pushed the English out of Burma, yet the whole of the British Empire lies just beyond the next mountain. We have swept the European powers from our seas, and yet this is just one ocean. The British navy is far from beaten. Even in this ocean, we are not alone." Now Tojo sat up. This is what he had been waiting for. The admiral continued, "Beyond the next wave lies America."

A commander at the end of the table arose and waited to be acknowledged. "I have heard what our grand admiral has said. I agree that much remains to be done. But I do not share the admiral's concern for America. They are a weak and selfish people. They only care about themselves and would never allow their sons to be sent against us."

Agreements were voiced, and then Tojo stood up. "With our navy lies our greatest strength and our greatest weakness. Our shipping is our life line; without it, we are finished. Our armies cannot fight without weapons or food. Our factories cannot run without fuel. Now that the Americans have cut off our oil, we have to take Malaysia to get more."

A voice from the end of the table said, "That will not be a problem. Our army could secure the oil within a month."

Tojo replied, "This is true, but could it take the country without the support of the navy?" No one answered. "So securing the oil would take a large commitment of our naval forces. And while our navy is off fighting, what will prevent the rather large American navy from sailing in and cutting them off?" Everyone could see the wisdom in their commander's words. Tojo continued, "We cannot allow the navy to sail off and leave our life lines unguarded. Without that oil, we are finished. Without our navy here to protect us, we are finished." As he sat down, a silence descended upon the council. In this global game of chess, they found themselves in check.

A young general stood up and said hesitantly, "We need the oil, but we cannot take it with a threat hanging over us. We must first remove the threat."

Tojo brought order back to the meeting and then looked at his reluctant admiral and said, "He is correct. You must develop a plan to remove this threat." Yammamotto stood and sadly accepted his orders.

*****

Billy had not enjoyed his first month in the army. Getting up at four thirty every morning had taken some getting used to. Marching up and down the parade area all day and standing at attention for hours on end was his whole world. He had been a soldier for almost five weeks and still had not seen a working gun. As they stood in line this morning, the heat had reached ninety degrees. Billy felt like he was going to pass out, when his sergeant finally walked out and gave them the order to march. Twenty minutes later, the group made a left-hand turn and headed for the rifle range. He felt a twinge of excitement. This was the first time they had come this way. Maybe now he would get his gun. The sergeant allowed the group to take a five-minute break, and they sat down on the sand and opened their canteens.

The stale water tasted like the greatest he had ever consumed. It wasn't long before the break was over and the platoon reassembled. His sergeant ordered them to form a line, and a new man walked out. After a five-minute review of the men, the soldier introduced himself as the commander of the target range. He then began a twenty-minute speech about the type of weapons they would be trained on and the proper way to conduct themselves while on his turf. He then ordered them into pairs and passed out small crates.

The pairs were to form a line, with one member of each pair holding the crate. The second man was to get down on his knees. In this formation, the group began searching the range for spent cartridges and any other trash they came across. When they reached the other end of the range, some three hundred yards away, they switched positions with their partners. After four hours of this, the platoon stood at attention and waited while each crate was inspected. They were marched back for lunch and then returned to the field an hour later. At this point, Billy was just going through the motions, when the sergeant began issuing rifles. This brought a small surge of excitement back to the platoon. They spent the remainder of the afternoon learning how to take apart their weapons and put them back together.

That evening, they marched back for supper, still sporting their rifles. As a matter of fact, they ate with them, showered with them, and slept with them. They spent the next four days perfecting the art of tearing apart, cleaning, and the reassembling their rifles. When they finally got to shoot them, Billy easily qualified as expert. There was a kind of grudge about finally being able to shoot the darn things.

After their first afternoon of target practice, several of the men could not find all of their spent cartridges. This led to a two-hour search, in the same mold as they had previously used for cleaning or, as the sarge called it, policing the range. After that, every cartridge was accounted for.

It was during this period that Billy received his first letter from LW. He ignored the first part, about how Katy had decided to leave him and run off with LW. He gave a grim smile at the second part: "So how are you enjoying camp? I'll bet you put on twenty pounds. With all that fishing, you're probably sunburned." In his return letter, Billy was sure to cast a golden glow on "camp."

Across the country, their cousin Henry was also thinking about LW and camp as he ran ankle-deep in the Mississippi swampland, batting at mosquitoes and cursing Billy with every step. The army was unlike any club he could have imagined. What he could not understand was why Billy didn't warn him. This was more like hell on earth. He still had not even seen a gun let alone shot one. He began to think that the army had installed him in some kind of sick experiment. Maybe they were trying to find out how much a man could take before it killed him. Henry had a sneaking suspicion that it wasn't much more. If he had to run like this for much longer, he'd be finished. He had not received a letter from home yet. But it wasn't because his family wasn't writing; it was because these satanic bastards wouldn't let him have them.

*****

By the time school started, LW and Doris were a serious item. They spent all the time they could together, much to the disappointment of her mother. Tonight was the big game. If they could beat Wichita, they would have a good chance of going on to state. LW was starting at middle linebacker, and he was having a tough evening. Doris was standing with the rest of the cheerleaders. The game was late in the fourth quarter, and they were leading 12–6. Wichita had the ball on Riverside's twelve-yard line. For the entire fourth quarter, Wichita had stuck with their all-state fullback. He relentlessly pounded the center of the Riverside defensive line. Play after play, yard by yard, they drove the length of the field.

LW had made tackle after tackle, and each one took a little more out of him. The fullback who seemed to always be heading his way outweighed him by at least forty pounds. The only thing keeping LW on his feet was anger. Each time they ran up the middle, he took it as a personal insult. They thought that they could pound him down. This made LW see red. As they snapped the ball, LW stepped up to meet the runner yet again. And yet again, the runner slammed into him and LW brought him to a stop at the ten-yard line. The blood that now began to run into LW's mouth only seemed to heighten his anger. In the huddle, the defenders spoke not a word, each one battle weary, each one standing on his last legs, each one determined not to be the weak link. Again, Wichita lined up, and the fullback headed for the center, and LW met him with the ferocity of a lion. Once more, the fullback went down, but this time it was to the six-yard line. For the first time, LW had been knocked on his back. It took him much longer to crawl to his knees than usual. As he tasted the blood and sweat that swirled in his mouth, he felt the frustration that can only come after a person has given everything and still it is not enough. He was shocked to find the runner in the same position as he was, on his hands and knees, spitting blood. As both stumbled to their feet, they looked each other in the eye and grudgingly nodded their respect.

LW looked up at the scoreboard and realized that it was third down. They had only two plays to go four yards. He felt he could hold him under that. With a Herculean effort, he willed strength back into his legs. What had escaped his attention was the clock. It was down to just twelve clicks, and Wichita had only one time-out remaining. As they came to the line, the fans came to their feet in a screaming fury. The sound on the field was deafening as the quarterback began his calls. LW locked his eyes on the fullback as the ball was snapped. He stepped forward to meet the charge. The ball was placed on the four-yard line as Wichita called it's last time-out. The fans were out of their minds with delight. They were witnessing an incredible finish to an incredible game.

The offense lined up for what could be the final snap. Again the fullback headed for the center, with his head down and legs churning. The thunderous crash echoed up and down the field as the two met again. LW felt that he had held him under two yards as he looked up to see the fullback smiling back at him. "What are you smiling about? I stopped you from getting the first down."

The fullback continued to smile. "You sure did, and a heck of a tackle it was. The only problem is, I don't have the ball." He held up his empty hands to emphasize his point. LW stood up and looked around in confusion. Lucky for him, his cornerback had no such problems. He saw the fake and moved up to meet the quarterback, who was running around his end. Normally, he would take out the back in this situation, but all the linebackers had gone for the fake and he was all alone. His only chance was to take out the quarterback and try to mess up the pitch that was sure to come. The safety had seen the fake too late to stop the quarterback but perhaps in time to stop the runner. The corner slammed into the quarterback only to see him flip out a wobble pitch. This wobble pitch caused the ball to go off course and slowed down the runner just a fraction of a second. This allowed the safety to meet the runner on the one-yard line and send him flying over the cone in the corner of the end zone. His foot went out about two feet from the end zone, just before the ball crossed the goal line. The clock stopped with one second left. They had picked up their first down and now had time for one more play. Every one in the stadium knew what that one play was going to be. This time, LW did not wait for the handoff but zoomed toward the back field in a mad blitz. Too late to change direction, the full back saw him fill the hole and lowered his head to meet the crazed linebacker. The impact was the same as before; however, this time it happened s two yards behind the line. LW held on with everything he had left as he was dragged toward the end zone. Finally, the fullback ran out of steam and fell. The ball ended up eight inches from the goal line.

As the stadium erupted into chaos, the defense that had performed so brilliantly lay stunned. LW, who was semiconscious, cared only that the game was finally over. The mighty fullback cared about nothing; that final blow had been too much. He was out cold. The doctor fought his way through the boisterous fans until he eyed the fallen combatants. Both boys were being picked up by various teammates and acted surprised when the old physician ordered them to lay them back down. After a brief check, the doctor swiped smelling salt under LW's nose and did the same to the fullback. Both boys responded to the offending smell and began to stir.

LW would finally come to in his bedroom the following morning. His headache would keep him in bed for all of the next day. A parade of teammates, coaches, family, friends, and well-wishers kept him and his parents occupied. Around lunchtime, Doris made her appearance. With an apple pie in one hand and a fork and napkin in the other, she shyly entered his room. It marked the first time that she had entered the exotic world of a boy's room, other than her brother's. LW had been complaining all day about his prescribed bed rest, but now he played up his injury as though he had but moments to live. His father had to hide a smile as he watched his son's performance. With two women fawning over him, LW was in heaven. Doris hand-fed him apple pie while his mother placed a cool rag upon his forehead.

"Does it hurt much?" Doris asked sweetly.

"Yes, but it's getting better," LW said with his mouth full. His father stood at the door, watching all that transpired. Standing next to him was Doris's father, who had arrived with his daughter. The fact that his wife had voiced her opinion against the visit had been outweighed by his daughter's pleas and his appreciation for LW's performance. Now, as he sat watching the interaction between the two young people, he saw what his wife had been trying to tell him. This was not a passing phase; this was something deeper. He liked the boy and his parents, but it was hard to accept that his daughter was growing up. Watching her feeding the obviously pleased boy made his heart hurt. This was his little girl, and now, for the first time, he could see the lady she was to become.

LW Sr. sensed what was behind the other man's frown.

"It's hard to watch them grow up, isn't it?" he said gently.

"Yes, yes it is," Doris's father responded. He then entered the room and shook LW's hand.

"Great game, LW. That last hit was one game-saving play." LW did not know how to take the appearance of this man, especially since Doris was sitting on his bed, feeding him apple pie. But the look in her father's eyes was one of pride, and LW felt a little more confident.

"Thank you, sir. I just wish that I could remember it." This brought laughter to everyone in the room.

The feelings of victory were doused a week later when LW's team was upset in their first play-off game. LW had a decent game, but it was not enough to counter the mistakes that were made, and they lost 17–10.

With the football season over and Thanksgiving around the corner, LW began to enjoy more and more time with Doris. The two of them became inseparable, even though her mother tried to keep them apart. Both of them managed to get through Thanksgiving without seeing each other. And as the calendar turned to December, they decided that they would not be separated during the next holiday.

Just before he was supposed to pick up Doris for their date that Saturday night, his mother handed him a letter from Billy. In the letter, Billy described army life after basic training. He discussed how he had learned to fire mortars and the intense training on the live fire course. Now this sounded more like it!

Though his cousin talked about the rigid discipline, massive amount of marching and running, and putting up with orders, it sounded like his situation was pretty good overall. Billy had had his time extended for six months, and he was in the final month of that extension. The letter said that he expected to be home shortly after the new year. He wrote that he had spent the last month learning how to hit hostile beaches. Billy described climbing down the rope nets on the side of big ships and getting into smaller crafts. He went on to brag that his commanding officer said that they were now the best trained unit in the entire army. He also went on to mention that he had qualified as an expert marksman and was now in training to be the squad's sniper.

LW smiled as he folded the letter and put it in his drawer. He made a mental note to write back soon. His father had told how important letters from home were to soldiers. He looked at the date on the letter and saw that it was written shortly after Thanksgiving, and the calendar on the wall showed the date December 6, 1941. He could afford to wait until tomorrow, considering that the mail did not run until Monday. And without another thought, he headed out the door and drove to Doris's house.

LW had trouble staying awake in church that morning. He had sat up late into the night responding to his cousin's letter. Now the preacher was going on and on about the evils of fascism and how the devil was pulling strings all over the world. LW got an elbow in the ribs for snoring during the sermon. The preacher looked right into his eyes and said, "The devil is after your soul." LW thought that if the devil was engaged with other matters around the world, he had little time to worry about little ol' LW. Even if he only heard a small portion of the preacher's words, the fact that he remained awake during the remaining forty-five minutes was considered a great achievement.

He had decided to go fishing that afternoon and was just getting his gear together when he heard his father turn up the radio. The words were clearly audible to him in his room. It seemed that something big was happening and it sounded like the president was talking. As he walked out into the living room, he barely noticed his parents sitting there, glued to the radio.

"I am going fishing. See you later," LW said. This brought no response, so halfway out the door, he stopped, turned, and looked at his parents for the first time. Both of them were staring at the radio. His mother had tears running down her face, and his father seemed to be in another world. Just then, the words of the president sunk in. "Did he just declare war on Japan?" LW asked.

His father looked at him and seemed to see him for the first time. "The Japanese just attacked Pearl Harbor," his father stated.

This was all too much. "What is Pearl Harbor?" he asked.

"It's not a what; it's a where. Pearl Harbor is our naval base in Hawaii. It's home to the Pacific fleet," his father replied.

"What does this mean?" LW asked.

"It means that we are at war."

Chapter Five

Billy was mad: mad at the Japanese, mad at the navy, and just mad in general. He had been informed that his duty had been extended yet again. This time, when he inquired about how long, the answer was not reassuring. The only thing he was told was that his time in the army was extended indefinitely. To add insult to injury, his troop was put on seventy-two-hour lock down. This meant that not only did they have to stay on base, but they had to remain in or around their barracks.

It was about twelve hours into the lockdown when their sergeant walked in and informed them that they had fifteen minutes to pack. They were moving out. He repeated the order in a much louder voice, drowning out all questions. Billy cleaned out his locker and picked up his gun. As he walked by his friend Jeff Grainger, he smiled and said, "War is hell, right?" Jeff laughed and finished tying his boots. Billy walked out just as the trucks were pulling up, so he threw his bag in and climbed up. He found a good spot right by the cab of the truck and sat down on the bench. Within minutes, the truck rolled out, and Billy settled in and went to sleep.

When he awoke, the sergeant was yelling at them again, and the squad jumped out and lined up. One thing was clear: they were up in the mountains. They were ordered to stack their rifles and grab a shovel and sandbags. Billy was wondering just where on this mountain of rock they would find sand. It was then that he noticed the dump trucks dropping sand on the road. They spent the next six hours building machine gun nests and road blocks.

His sergeant came up to him and ordered him to climb up the mountain and locate a spot where he could see the beach. Two other men were ordered to join him. One carried a radio, and the other carried a spotting scope. Each of the three men carried two full sandbags. This made the climb very tiring, as well as dangerous. Billy had to climb for an hour, following sheep trails and troughs cut by rain. Finally, he found a perch with a breathtaking view. Not only could he see the beach but he could see for miles in almost every direction.

"What are we supposed to do now?" asked one of the soldiers.

"Sit up here and watch the beach," the other soldier replied.

Billy was taking careful aim with his prized thirty-ought-six. He half listened to the conversation going on around him. One thing he knew for sure: there was no way he could effectively hit a target on the road beneath them, let alone one on the beach. None of the machine gun nests they had built were anywhere near the water. With that thought in my mind, Billy turned and looked back at the area below him. What he saw was a full-fledged army camp that had not been there this morning. The soldiers looked like little ants. He knew that the holes they were digging would be lined with sandbags and filled with ammo. After three hours, they saw an anti-aircraft column headed north, in the general direction of Los Angeles. A cruiser sailed by, though it was hard to make out. This caused a few moments of excitement as the radio man called headquarters and then waited for the positive ID. Billy figured that the Japs would send more than a cruiser. It turned out to be one of their own. They were finally relieved and headed down from their nest and went to explore their new home.

*****

Henry was flabbergasted. How on earth had he gotten himself into this? All he had wanted to do was serve out his one year in relative peace. In his mind, he had served his time. It was not his fault that the army had extended his duty. And now there was a real war going on.

Henry sat in his Sherman tank, watching the rain fall. His unit had been deployed close to Washington DC, but not close enough to see anything of the town. He understood the necessity of the deployment, but the fact that they were so close to the capital caused no small amount of alarm. He could not believe that anyone could attack Washington. Maybe by air, maybe even by ship, but certainly not by land. And if the powers that be thought it a possibility, then maybe they were in more trouble than they thought. He voiced his opinion to another tank commander. The other man chewed on this a minute and then said, "They would have to come in force. I mean, it would take a lot of ships to fight their way through our navy. The Germans don't have much of a surface fleet, and the Japs would hit the West Coast not the East. No, most likely it's just a precaution."

Henry looked at him and asked, "Why would the Germans matter? We aren't at war with them."

The other soldier looked at him a moment and said, "Haven't you been listening to the radio? Germany declared war on us two hours ago."

Henry was appalled. He had figured he might get out of the war in the Pacific. There was not much use for big tank divisions on those islands. But Europe was a totally different ballgame. There was plenty of room for tanks and plenty of German tanks to shoot at them. He thought about LW then, how he was probably out fishing. Henry sure wished that he could be there with him.

*****

LW was sitting on his front porch, lost in thought. Christmas was approaching, and he grew more anxious by the day. He had to pick out a suitable present for Doris. No matter how hard he tried, he could not shake the sense of sadness he felt. There was a war going on, and his two cousins could find themselves right in the middle of it. His life had changed so quickly, it seemed like just yesterday he and his cousins were going fishing together.

Doris found him sitting in a lawn chair, looking up at the stars. LW barely acknowledged her presence. She reached out and held his hand. They sat like this for some time before LW finally spoke. "You know they might never come back. People are going to be shooting at them and trying to kill them."

Doris started to cry as he went on. "I think this war may take a long time, and we will probably lose a lot of people. I don't think we will ever get back to the way it was."

Doris answered in a quiet voice. "At least we still have each other. My brother left for the army today." She started crying even harder.

LW had forgotten about her brother. He was at a loss for words. The truth was, he felt the same way. Both of them felt their stomachs turn at the thought of the loss of their loved ones.

Christmas was a solemn affair. News about the war was coming in fast now. On every front, the Allies were being thrown back. The Japanese were taking city after city. In Europe, the Germans seemed unstoppable.

The new year brought further misery to LW. The Philippines had fallen, and Billy had been sent off to an unknown location. LW was trying to concentrate on his upcoming Golden Gloves fight. He had won the city championship and was fighting for the area title.

The morning of the fight, he found his thoughts far away from the ring. His father drove him to the building two hours before the scheduled match. After they entered the locker room, LW Sr. slapped LW.

"What was that for?" LW asked.

"Because your mind is not where it should be. If you go into the ring like this, you will be clobbered," his father replied sharply. The painful lesson left its mark on LW's mind as well as his cheek. It was a lesson that would stay with him and serve him well for the rest of his life. Tonight, though, it served to focus his mind on the task at hand.

When the fight started, Doris was sitting in the first row with LW Sr. She was horrified at the animalistic ferocity on display just a few feet away.

LW was having a time of it. His opponent was throwing jab after jab, backing LW up. He had landed more than a few on LW's nose, which was beginning to drip blood. Each and every time LW moved in, he found that jab in his face. He was starting to get frustrated, when finally, in the sixth round, he managed to land a left hook. The blow stunned his opponent long enough for LW to land a right to the body followed by a left uppercut to an unprotected chin. The crowd was on its feet, and so was the fighter, though he was totally unaware of his surroundings. A solid jab from LW ended the fight.

His father met him in the locker room and could not control his enthusiasm. "That was a beautiful fight. I thought he was going to wear you down for a minute there." LW was too tired to respond. His nose was hurting and his legs felt like rubber.

He stood in the shower for twenty minutes, letting the hot water cascade over his head. Earlier, he had taken some aspirin and had sat still while the doctor carefully checked him over. Now his mind was clear, and he just wanted to remain under the warm embrace of the flowing water. He could hear his father conferring with his manager. Their voices were muffled and barely registered in his exhausted mind. Too soon for the weary fighter, the voices died out and he knew it was time to dry off. When he emerged from the shower, he found the locker room deserted. Pleased at the silence that engulfed the room, LW sat down and began to dress.

He felt a strange sensation and realized that he was feeling lonely. In his previous fights, his cousins had been waiting for him, ready with smart comments and jokes. He could almost hear them, teasing him about his swollen nose.

Unbeknownst to LW, his father had entered the room and now stood there silently. He saw the vacant look in his son's eyes and the wistful smile on his lips. He felt his heart melt as he realized what his son was feeling. "You know, that was really a terrific punch," he said.

LW was caught off guard and wiped his eyes. "I had to wait long enough to find an opening."

His father smiled as he sat down next to him. "All that matters is that you did find that opening. You know, LW, people come and go, but the ones who really matter will always be with you. No matter what happens in the future, no matter who dies or who lives, the feelings you have for your cousins will always be there. The only real truth is that no one gets out of this world alive."

Tears had begun to flow out of LW's eyes. "Then what's the point? If everyone you care about leaves, what's the point?"

Now it was his father's turn to smile. "That's what I am trying to tell you. What matters is the time that you spend with the people you care about. The point is the memories. That's all anyone can take with them, and they are more precious than gold. As you get older, you begin to lose the people who mean the world to you. First your grandparents and then your parents. As you lose them, other people will begin to take their place. In time, you will get married and have children; then your children will have children. It's just one big circle, never ending. From time to time, people fall off the circle and others come to fill the empty voids. If you're lucky, and few people are, you will live to be an old man. Your body will wither, and every friend and relative that you grew up with will be long gone. Only two things will remain for you: your younger family members and your memories. Someday, I will be gone, and the only thing left of me will be your memories—yours and those of your children. But because of those memories, I'll never really be gone. That's the point. Those are the ties that bind. No matter what happens, your cousins will always be there, in your heart, and nothing can take that from you."

LW saw the logic in his father's words, but that didn't make things any easier. "You know, Dad, it won't be long before I have to go away, too."

"Maybe not; the war maybe over by then." Both men sat silently, sharing this moment that would soon be just a memory. A knock on the door interrupted their reflections.

"It's Doris," LW stated.

"Take your time. I'll go keep her busy."

"Thanks, Dad."

"You bet."

LW began lacing up his shoes. Before the door closed, he heard his father tell Doris that he was just finishing up. He smiled as he threw his towel in his bag and walked out the door. As the door closed, silence again settled over the room. It was an old room that had undoubtedly seen many scenes like this, which were hopelessly lost in time. For just a brief second, the room seemed to pause, as if to capture forever in its walls the emotions that were shared between father and son. And then the water in the shower began to drip and time moved on.

By the beginning of spring, LW and Doris were a permanent item. Both now believed that they had found their soul mate. Both sets of parents had come to the same conclusion and vowed to keep them separate as much as possible, and failing that, at least reduce the time they spent alone. Though all four parents agreed on the seriousness of the relationship, their reasons for wanting to keep the two separate were different. LW's parents, along with Doris's father, were concerned about intimacy, while Doris's mother was more concerned with LW. She had decided long ago that LW was not the boy for her daughter and set out to destroy the relationship. The futility of this endeavor would in time become self-evident. And instead accepting it, she would turn it into a lifelong grudge. LW shrugged it off and continued his courtship without a second thought.

*****

Billy could not believe what he was seeing. There must have been thousands of people on the beach. He and his squad members had been given weekend leave. They had decided to spend it in Los Angeles. Their first mission was to find a place to sleep. This was not an easy task considering that the city had swelled to twice its size as military personnel from the army and navy swarmed in. They finally found a widow who rented them two rooms. With this taken care of, they set off in search of some local wildlife. It didn't take long to find their way down to the beach. Billy had stopped at the post office and sent six letters that he had written while he was stuck on that mountain ledge. Now that they were sitting on the beach and drinking beer, their time in the mountain pass was slowly forgotten. Billy lay there, relaxed, remembering the trip his family had taken to the Grand Canyon. Both of his cousins and their families had gone with them.

The massive canyon had been impressive but paled in comparison to the spectacle of LW Sr. desperately clinging to an enraged donkey. LW Sr. was a tall man; his feet were just touching the ground, giving the appearance of a giant dragging his feet while riding a pygmy horse. With his feet dragging on the ground and his hat thrown off, he looked very much like a circus clown, so much so that his wife was at a loss for words. She was scared to death for her husband and was doing her best to express herself; at the same time, she was trying not to laugh. It didn't take long for her husband to disappear down the trail, leaving behind a dusty and shocked group of spectators.

LW, for his part, had never laughed so hard in his life. Watching his father fly down the canyon, his pale, bald head reflecting sunlight like a calm pond on a bright morning, left him holding his side and desperate for air. His own donkey was becoming confused; his rider was leaning way over on one side and making a horrible noise. LW, still fighting for breath, was trying to get control of his donkey and keep from following in his father's path, when his mother began pounding him on top of his head. This was too much for the poor little beast to endure. He let loose with a fury of kicks and screams and then raced off to join his companion down the trail. LW clung on for dear life. His mother could be heard yelling, "Serves you right." Realizing both her husband and son were now in mortal danger, she too bolted down the trail.

Their guide, who was now flabbergasted at the sudden desertion of half his herd, started yelling at the rest of the group. Henry wasn't sure what language their little guide was using, and he never found out. His father was already in a foul mood. He had not wanted to spend his vacation in the middle of the desert. He really didn't want to do it camping out, and most assuredly, he did not wish to spend two hours on the back of a donkey. He hated everything about this trip, including the foreigner who was their guide. He despised Latin, though his wife assured him the man's language was not Latin. "Then what language is it," Henry's father demanded.

"I don't know, but I do know it is not Latin."

"You wouldn't know Latin if it bit you in the butt," he replied angrily.

Before she could retort, LW Sr.'s donkey went berserk, which immediately brought about a laughing fit from her husband. As a matter of fact, all the male members of their party were in tears—all, that is, except their little Spanish-speaking guide. He sat there, stunned, and watched as not one but three of his donkeys went rampaging down the canyon trail. He knew how steep the trail was and that a fall would be fatal. The guide had no idea what the punishment for allowing a man to fall off the canyon rim would be. But he had no illusions about his fate if a little boy and her mother fell. My God, the authorities might think he was trying to knock off the whole party. He immediately began to panic, yelling at the top of his lungs, trying to establish his authority over the remaining burrows. The animals were ready to bolt down the trail.

It was at this critical juncture that the big, burly American entered the picture. Henry heard his father exclaim, "By God, that's enough," and then he hit the little guide, knocking him over the rear of his donkey. The guide was now rolling dangerously toward the edge, when Henry jumped of his donkey and came to his rescue. Both donkeys, now free of their riders, broke at a dead run down the trail.

LW Sr. had no clue what had sent the mad beast on its bone-jarring rampage. All he knew was that he was being carried toward the bottom of the canyon at an uncontrollable speed. When the animal finally came to a stop, it was a sudden, shocking stop. Unable to hold onto anything but the reins, he went flying over the donkey's ears and landed in the river. He stood up, spitting water and swearing vengeance on the world. Then he noticed his hat sitting on the bank and watched as the donkey began to chew on it. Soaking wet, tired, and completely dazed, he reached over and jerked his hat out of the animal's mouth and then punched it on the nose. About that time, he heard a flood of cuss words followed by the sudden appearance of his son, who was miraculously able to perform the exact same dismounting technique as his father.

LW landed within three feet of his irate dad. But instead of landing on his back, he performed the much more difficult maneuver of a frontal dismount, flying headfirst into the river. His father grabbed LW by his hair and stood him up. Unbelievably, LW was spouting cuss words and water at the same time. It was at that moment that his mother made her appearance. Seeing that both her men were alive and relatively unharmed, she relaxed and made a much more dignified, but far less impressive, dismount. She immediately corrected LW for his language and then bent down and began washing her hands and face in the river. There was another commotion, and two more donkeys arrived with empty saddles. LW Sr. stared at them a moment and then said, "Now ain't that peculiar."

His wife looked up and then covered her mouth and said, "You don't think they fell off the trail, do you?"

"I didn't hear anyone scream, and I don't see any bodies lying around here," LW Sr. replied.

"What a terrible thing to say."

"It's the truth. I mean, we are right under them. If they fell, we would have seen or heard something," LW Sr. stated.

His wife looked up, disgusted. "That's still a terrible thing to say."

LW didn't see a problem with his father's logic. He did, however, see a problem with his mother's response to his foul language. LW went about gathering the now placid donkeys. They eyed him with suspicion but seemed to want to be close to humans. LW did not trust the beasts at all. In his mind, they had betrayed him when he needed them the most.

Billy spied his cousin standing with the donkeys and could not stop his mouth from getting him in trouble. "Somebody better go get those jackasses before they wander off." Everyone laughed; even LW's mother smiled at the remark. Their guide immediately went to his wayward flock and gave LW a grateful look.

Henry asked, "Should we make camp here?"

The guide turned and said, "Not here. We must find higher ground."

"Are we expecting an Indian attack?" LW Sr. asked.

"No, señor, we are preparing for rain," the guide answered patiently.

Billy was unaware of the smile that came over him as he lay stretched out in the warm California sun. He was brought back from his daydreaming by a sudden cold burst of water. He jumped up and ran after the girl who had thrown the bucket, and memories of yesterday were again memories.

*****

LW stood silently in his living room. His father had a distant look upon his face, and his mother was sobbing uncontrollably. LW did not know what to say. He had expected a much different reaction than the one he was witnessing. He thought his father would be more supportive and his mother more heroic and both of them would be beaming with pride. He had joined the navy, and what's more, he had joined the navy air program. His mother was falling to pieces right before his eyes. LW was set to graduate high school in a week. He knew he would be drafted. His father finally looked up and grabbed a hold of his arm.

"You did right, son. It was a smart move."

His mother did not agree "How can you say that? He's just a boy."

"He's not a boy any longer. Besides, it is far better to enlist than it is to be drafted."

She gave her husband a venomous look. "How's that?"

"Look, if he had been drafted, then they would have placed him wherever they wanted. Army, marine corps, wherever. Now they have to put him in the navy air program. At least until he flunks out. And he has to go to basic training, officer's candidate school, flight training. It could be years of training in the States."

His mother saw a ray of hope and grasped it desperately. "You must promise me, LW. Promise me that you won't flunk out."

LW did not like the way the conversation was turning, and he was alarmed by the desperation in his mother's voice. "I promise. Do you think I am stupid or something?"

"No, LW, I am not worried about your grades. I am worried about you getting into trouble."

"Now why would you worry about that?" LW said with a smile.

His mother was in no mood to joke around. She hit him squarely in the arm. "I mean it, LW. This is not funny. You will be on your best behavior and you will graduate."

He could not resist. "I am graduating, in one week."

His mother gave him a feeble slap on the arm and crushed him to her. "No matter how big you get, you'll always be my baby." He turned red and quietly took his mother's embrace.

LW stood smiling in his cap and gown. Doris, who was a grade behind him, sat happily with his parents. LW was leaving for basic training in three days.

He spent the remaining time either comforting his mother or Doris or both. It got to be such a burden that he was ecstatic when the time came for him to leave. His father had to almost pry him away from the two women, who were acting like it was the last time they would ever see him. LW smiled and waved good-bye from the train. He was so thankful for the reprieve that he did not even feel nervous. Compared to the rest of the boys on the train, LW was an island of contentment.

Chapter Six

Billy had enjoyed his time laying in the California sunshine. It had certainly been better than being crowded on board a troop transport. He had no idea where they were heading; nobody else seemed to either. They had reported in every day while on leave. When their orders had finally come, they had been ready to go. Now, floating somewhere in the Pacific, Billy began to regret not doing more while on leave. At first, he had been excited at the prospect of battle. That had slowly turned to anxiety over a period of a week. The fact was that he was just plain bored. He was even hoping for a storm, anything to break the monotony. When a storm finally came, he found himself begging for the bored calm of the previous week. Waves thirty feet in height rocked the transport. Vomit and sea water covered everything. All the soldiers were sick. There was water everywhere: in the hold, cascading down the hatches, pouring over the sides of the ship. He was pretty sure the ship was sinking. The storm lasted for just over ten hours. They spent another three hours cleaning up the vomit.

Billy sat on the stern of the ship, staring out over the vast empty sea. Far away, he could see the mast of another war ship. He thought that it was kind of odd that the convoy was so spread out. He asked a passing sailor why this was. The sailor seemed to want to ignore him, but finally turned and replied, "We separated during the storm in order not to be smashed into one another. The convoy is almost reformed."

Billy thanked him and sat contemplating this, when another thought crossed his mind: it was getting cold, very cold. His platoon had been training in the desert for the last year and were not used to cold weather. Not that the desert didn't get cold at night, but nothing like this.

It was about this time that Bud, a private first class, walked up and asked, "Say, Billy, what's that white thing floating out there?" Billy had to squint to see it, but Bud was right; there was something floating out there. He thought it might be a target or maybe a whale. He was just getting up for a better view when a big chunk of ice came sliding by.

"Ice! There's ice in the water!" Bud exclaimed.

Billy went to find his captain and report the incredible discovery. "Captain, you're not going to believe what we saw. There's ice in the water."

His captain barely heard him as he read over his recently received orders. "The Aleutians. We're going to the Aleutians. Where the hell is that?" the captain asked nobody in particular. Turning, he saw Billy and repeated the question.

"I don't know but I think it's near the North Pole," Billy answered.

The captain, now even more confused, replied, "What makes you think that?"

Billy held down his impatience "That's what I have been saying. There's ice floating in the water."

"Ice? Why is there ice?"

"Because we are so far north."

The captain started screaming for a map, and after a moment, he found the islands. All the men in the room gathered around. One of the men asked, "What's on those islands?"

The captain answered, "The Japs are."

Billy thought that he had never been so cold in all his life. There was ice on his gloves, on the rope, and even on the ladder they would soon descend. The men huddled together, trying to stay warm. The waves were splashing over their landing crafts twenty feet below. All the men stood quietly, each lost in their own contemplation of what they were about to do. The whistle sounded, and three hundred men began climbing down the ice-covered ladders. As Billy took his turn and began to climb down, he heard the air warnings go off. There was nothing to do but keep climbing down. The ship was caught in the middle of launching the first assault wave and could not take evasive action. Billy was halfway down the ladder when he heard the plane come in just above the deck. He saw the flash of its gun and could clearly see the rising sun insignia on its wings. The landing craft on the stern side of the ship exploded in a hail of machine gun fire. The entire area of the ship all around the stricken craft was splattered with blood. Billy and the rest of the third platoon were shocked at the speed in which death had found them. Their friends, who they had worked and played with, who just minutes ago they had shared breakfast with, were gone. In the blink of an eye, their world had changed. The suffering and death of armies and civilians around the world were no longer just images; they had entered the unforgiving and unmerciful playing field of death and destruction.

The captain began, yelling and their training took over. In seconds, the entire third platoon was standing in their craft. They were the first boat to get free of their moorings and head toward the beach. The air around them was swarming with rounds and shrapnel. They could hear the *rat tat tat* of machine guns and the clangs as metal slammed itself against the hull of their boat. Then there was the bone-jarring jerk as their craft hit ground and came to a sudden stop. "Get off the boat! Get off the boat!" the captain yelled again and again. Billy hesitated a moment and then jumped overboard.

The freezing water slammed into him and left him gasping for breath. The shore was only a hundred feet away, but the cold water and the shock of being in combat made it seem like a mile. The bullets slapped the water as the gunners moved back and forth over the advancing army. Billy could see, though he took no notice of them at the time, other boats that had found themselves stranded. Billy finally struggled into knee-deep water and then collapsed behind the protection of a group of rocks. He noticed that his clip was empty and paused to reload. It struck him as interesting that he did not remember firing a single shot. The world was exploding all around him, and he felt like he was the only man left alive. Unbelievably, he could see other soldiers running on the beach. Some ran straight up the beach, but most seemed to be trying to find shelter from the storm raging all around them. Billy spied another group of rocks about twenty yards in front of him and made a mad dash for it. Bullets plowed the ground in a mad game of tag, trying without success to reach him before he made it to the shelter. Billy beat them by a mere fraction of an inch. As he lay in his new hiding place, he looked towards the water and was taken aback by what he saw. His boat was now a burning hulk of twisted metal and wood. His platoon, or at least half of it, lay floating in a grotesque line, marking their progress toward the beach. As he took stock of the situation, he became aware of the screams reverberating up and down the landing area. Everywhere he heard cries and calls for help. Frustrated by the wholesale slaughter of his friends, he became enraged.

He turned and began searching for targets just above the beach line. Finally, finding a helmet sticking up over a machine gun barrel, he took careful aim and knocked the helmet off. He repeated this process until his clip was empty and then reloaded and began again. Billy became lost to everything but the need to fire his weapon. His rifle clicked empty for the fifth time. Finding no more targets, Billy jumped over the rocks and headed up the beach. Just before he reached the enemy's position, he tossed a grenade up and over the short wall. He did not even slow down as he jumped over the palisade. Luckily, the grenade exploded moments before he came sliding down the far side of the bank. Seeing Billy run for the enemy lines caused the rest of the platoon to follow suit. He spotted a large gun sighting down on the second wave of assault boats and took careful aim. He shot the soldier trying to load the gun and then proceeded to wipe out the gun crew. The Japanese realized that their forward positions had been overrun and ordered their troops to fall back.

Billy could not see any more targets and finally gave up and sat down. As he looked around, he saw the ragtag band that was all that was left of their platoon.

"Where's the captain?" Billy inquired.

"He never made it out of the boat," Bud replied. Hearing this, the survivors tried to account for all their friends.

"What are we supposed to do now?" asked one of the bleary-eyed privates.

"Sit tight and wait for orders," Billy said firmly. No one felt like arguing with this mad man, who, in their darkest hour, had known what to do. Billy looked down at his watch and saw that more than three hours had passed since they had first began loading onto their boats.

Random fire suddenly struck the grass around them, and shells were exploding just a hundred yards inland. None of the soldiers even flinched. Billy sat drinking water. He could not seem to get enough of it.

"You know who would just eat this up? LW. That sick guy would just love this," Billy said.

"Who's LW?" Bud inquired.

"Oh, sorry. I was just thinking out loud. My cousin LW would just love this. He probably thought boot camp was heaven itself."

*****

LW was neck-deep in swamp water and was indeed having the time of his life. Some old marine was their drill sergeant, and every time he cussed at them, LW started grinning. The marine took this as an insult and cussed louder, at which LW's grin widened. However, his arms were getting tired and he felt like a wet mop. Their unit had been running through the swamps all day. And it looked like they would be doing it all night, as well. LW was like a kid in a candy shop. He saw some new, fascinating creature around every turn. He was watching carefully as a big snake hung precariously from a branch just above the old marine. The marine moved in front of LW to get in closer and drive his point home. The snake saw his opportunity and dropped down across the soldier's exposed neck. LW had waited for this moment in anticipation, and when it finally came, he exploded with laughter. The laughs died as the snake was pulled from the sergeant's neck and flung directly into the middle of the partially submerged group. Panic swept through the recruits, and the snake was given as much room as possible. Like a herd of stampeding beasts, the boys scrambled out of the mudhole and up the bank, only to be pushed back in. Their terror was only confounded when the object of their fears failed to reappear. After several minutes of turmoil, the boys began to settle down, though more out of exhaustion than discipline. Still, the whereabouts of the snake remained a mystery.

The sergeant was far too experienced to believe that the snake was staying under water of its own accord. Something or, more precisely, someone was preventing it from resurfacing. His eyes soon found the only sailor who didn't move during the entire episode. LW was standing quietly, eyes forward, lost in his own thoughts.

"Culver, what in the hell are you doing?" the drill sergeant yelled.

"Standing still like you told me to, sir," LW calmly replied.

"Did you see where that snake went?"

"Into the water, sir."

"I know it went into the water; I threw it in. What I want to know is where it went after it hit the water."

"The water is muddy, sir. I didn't see it after it went under."

The old sergeant was at a loss for words, a problem he rarely had. He felt for certain that LW had had a hand in the snake's sudden disappearance, but how to prove it? Frustrated, he ordered the platoon to march out of the water and stand at attention. He then circled the hole, searching for the snake's escape route. Meanwhile, the snake suddenly found itself free and on dry land. Slithering toward a nearby bush, it was soon out of sight.

LW breathed a sigh of relief after the silent fight with the snake curled around his arm was won. He immediately resumed his dreamy stare, as if nothing in this world was out of place. The drill sergeant completed his inspection and moved onto a time-tested technique: interrogation. It took nearly ten minutes to get the story in its entirety. He ordered the platoon to march back to its barracks, with the exception of one sailor. After the platoon had left, the drill sergeant eyed his troublesome charge.

"You are a smart mouth, you know that!" It was a statement, not a question. LW wisely kept his mouth shut and his eyes forward.

"I think a night under the stars would be just what the doctor ordered." Again LW said nothing.

"You will stay here and guard this mudhole until I relieve you."

"Guard it against what?" LW asked sheepishly.

"Against snakes, that's what. Tomorrow I will take a mud bath, and I better not see any creatures in my mud."

"What about dinner?" LW questioned, growing concerned.

"You're so smart; I'm sure you can figure it out. You are not to leave sight of this hole, you understand."

"I understand perfectly," LW said with a slight edge to his voice. After a final stare, the drill sergeant stalked away.

LW could see the flashes of lightning off in the distance and judged he had an hour or less. Moving quickly through the snake-infested brush, he gathered all the vines he could. Finding three small trees growing within a few feet of each other, he quickly tied the limbs together. By weaving in branches that he cut from other trees, he soon had an igloo like hut. He gathered half-dry mud from the mudhole and created a ring in the center of the hut. Then he began to collect dried sticks and leaves. The rain was getting closer. The night had become still. He judged it to be close to eight o'clock.

He began to rub a stick against a larger branch, soon grinding it faster and faster. He rubbed his hands together, spinning the stick back and forth until a thin ribbon of smoke appeared. After a while— what felt like forever in LW's mind—a tiny glowing ember fell off and landed in his pile of dried leaves. He gently began to blow, occasionally using his hands to fan the ember. Soon a faltering flame could be seen. He quickly fed it small twigs and leaves. Then he added bigger and bigger sticks, until a raging fire sat in the center of his ring of mud. He sat for a moment and enjoyed his handy work. A loud thunder clap brought him back to the problems at hand. He grumbled about the unfair treatment. Staying out all night was more of a holiday than a punishment, but being left without food or the means to acquire it was just plain mean.

He stumbled back into the brush in search of more wood. The rain was closing in. He figured he had another five minutes at best. Spying a large dead bush, he smiled. There lay all the firewood he would need. Just as he walked up to it, a small black figure came crawling out. Caught completely off guard, both man and beast stared at each other. Standing not two feet apart, neither was in a position to take the high road and retreat. The dark shadow was the first to move. Roaring ferociously, it attacked. LW was shocked. A moment ago, he was happy and content, delighted in his abilities. Now he was in a life or death struggle with an unknown and apparently vicious creature. The battle was hard-fought and short. The creature bit, clawed, and kicked while LW stomped, punched, and stabbed with his navy-issued survival knife. The roars of the animal were met by the screams and cusses of the man. Finally, the victor stood over his prize and breathed a sigh of relief. LW noticed that a light sprinkle had begun to fall, and reaching down, he carefully picked up his opponent and retreated to his hut. Dropping his trophy near the fire, he smiled as he saw that it was a large male possum. Dinner had walked right into his lap.

Hearing the sprinkle turn into big drops of rain, he hurried back to the bush and brought in three armfuls of dried wood. He then headed out to get the last of his shopping supplies: five green branches and a large, flat rock. The rock was placed in the center of his fire, the mud circle having hardened with the heat, and the branches were woven together to make a crude but adequate door. Using the last of his vines, he tied the door up at the top, middle, and bottom, creating hinges. He then tied the door in the middle of the opposite side, effectively locking it. He went to work gutting and skinning the possum. After removing the entrails, head, and tail and throwing them as far as possible, he cut the animal in two and placed it on his flat stone. Soon the hut began to fill with the aroma of cooking meat. LW enjoyed his meal and lay back on a bed of leaves, picking his teeth with a stick and listening to the rain. His hut had a few leaks, but beyond that, it was perfect. Warm and dry, he drifted off into a deep slumber, dreaming of a girl and milkshakes.

LW awoke feeling refreshed and satisfied. He noticed that his fire had burned down to coals and added more sticks. Once his fire was attended to, he put his boots on, being careful to shake them out first, and unsealed his lair. It was still dark outside but LW knew it was close to sunrise. Already darkness had begun to give way to light. Lightning in the distance held the promise of more rain to come, and LW hurried to find a decent restroom. Two bushes growing a short distance away proved to be just what he was looking for. A light mist was still falling, and fog seemed to be edging in. On the way back to his hut, he noticed a familiar shape gliding in front of him. Smiling, LW caught the unlucky snake and stood studying it. He began to hear footsteps, his relief was coming. Hurrying inside his hut, he threw the remainder of the possum back on the rock and stretched back.

The sergeant did not sleep well; thoughts of the sailor left stranded and alone in the woods kept him smiling all night. Now he was practically running to reach the mudhole. He imagined the recruit soaked to the skin and scared to death. He was in such a hurry this morning that he skipped early chow. The pleasure of seeing his smart-mouthed recruit cowering and exhausted was worth delaying breakfast. Funny, he didn't realize how hungry he was. Now it seemed his mouth was watering, and he thought he could smell something cooking. The smell became stronger the closer he got to the mudhole. Finally, he reached it, but the sailor was nowhere to be seen. He could hear what sounded like snoring coming from a large bush. Upon further inspection, he realized that it was a crude but well-built shelter and the source of the aroma that had aroused his stomach. He tried to open the door, but it wouldn't budge. Finally, with some effort, he managed to break through and enter. The inside was surprisingly warm, though smoky, and only slightly damp. He saw the fire and the bits of meat cooking, and then spied LW asleep in a pile of leaves. He smiled and then backed out of the hut and screamed, "Culver, front and center!" LW quickly emerged from the hut. He stood before his door and kept his eyes forward.

"I set you to guard this hole and I find you asleep."

"Sir, only two creatures made an attempt to retake the hole."

"Well, where are these creatures, private?"

"The first tried to make a frontal assault and was killed in action, sir."

"I see, and the second?"

"Caught and secured, sir." LW now held up the snake for inspection.

"Well done, private. Report for showers and chow."

"Aye, aye, sir." LW began to march off toward breakfast.

"Sailor, release that prisoner before you get back to base."

"Aye, aye, sir."

The sergeant waited until LW was well on his way before chuckling and entering the hut. He sat down on the leaf pile and picked up a hot piece of meat. He always did love possum.

That afternoon, LW was made platoon leader, and life for the rest of the platoon became unbearable. LW used every spare moment to remind them of his new position. The entire platoon, to a man, celebrated graduation day. It was during that afternoon, when each man was receiving his orders, that the drill sergeant informed LW that he was going to OCS.

"That's officer candidate school, LW," the marine said with a smile. "You're going to make one fine marine."

LW looked at him a moment and then replied, "You mean one fine navy pilot." The drill sergeant looked disgusted. "You mean I trained you for the navy? What a waste of time."

LW grinned, saluted, and walked away. His excitement was growing by the minute: OCS, if he could finish it, and then on to flight school. But more important, Billy and Henry would have to salute him. The thought brought him overwhelming joy. He could see himself arriving for Christmas, with all the family there, and walking into the room. Henry and Billy would have to jump up and salute their superior officer. This would be more than they could stand. But by law, they had to. *Wait a minute, Billy is overseas and it is only a matter of time until Henry joins him.* This thought brought despair. He had to hurry and graduate before Henry got away.

*****

If the briefing had been set up to scare the hell out of them, then the army had succeeded. Henry sat with his mouth open, shocked beyond words. The film they had just been shown was German war footage. Even if this was propaganda, the cold, hard facts were still there. The coordination on display between the artillery, air forces, and infantry had been stunning. Watching the attacking German forces quickly sweep aside the Polish defenders left an empty feeling inside the young, green, American tankers. The sergeant stood up after the lights came on and cleared his throat.

"Well as you can see, the Germans are unstoppable. They have better training, far better equipment, and better leadership than we do. They are seasoned fighters. We haven't fought a war in twenty-plus years. So do you have any idea what's going to happen when we finally meet them on the field?"

He looked into the eyes of each of his tankers. After waiting the appropriate amount of time, he answered his own question. "We are going to kick their teeth down their throats. And do you know why?" Again the sergeant had to give the answer.

Henry had absolutely no idea how the Germans could possible lose. "Because, we are going to train night and day, seven days a week, until we are a well-oiled machine. Because we are Americans, and we have never lost a war. And, finally, because we are in the right, and God is on our side."

As soon as the sergeant finished his speech, the room erupted into cheers, everyone pounding each other on the back like they had just reached Berlin. Henry sat quietly absorbing the scene around him. He had heard that kind of speech before, many, many times. It was always delivered in the same way and always by the same person: LW. He gave it every time he talked Henry into doing something that he shouldn't and didn't want to do.

Later that day, Henry sat with a stop watch, watching his gunner take in more ammo. He was bound and determined to do exactly as the sergeant said: practice night and day. Over the following weeks, Henry worked his tank and crew nonstop. Darkness was the only thing that his crew could look forward to. Henry solved this problem by rigging up two truck headlights to his tank. Thus began what Henry called night practice. He even went so far as making his crew lift weights made from an old axle, two buckets, and concrete. They burned through hundreds of rounds, twelve tracks, and two engines. When the week of testing came around, his crew finished first in every category. The following day, Henry was called into the division commander's office and told he was being promoted and given command over two other tanks. Henry's thoughts were not on his promotion but on the awesome responsibility he had been given. His commander had mistakenly thought that Henry's pushing his crew was driven from the desire to be the best. Though this was true, he wanted to be the best out of fear, not out of pride. Now the thought of two inexperienced crews under his command brought on pure panic. Henry began working his tanks at a feverish pace. A month later, his crews finished first, second, and third in the next test.

They were informed that they would be given a month's leave before shipping out. Rumor had it that this was the big deployment. They were finally going to give the Nazis a little taste of their own medicine. Henry bought his ticket home and began to pack. He hoped LW and Billy would be there.

*****

LW had not only graduated OCS, he had actually excelled. He didn't finish top of his class by any means but was at least in the top ten. His next orders were to attend flight school in Pensacola. He had three weeks before he had to report for duty. LW bought his ticket and headed home. It was nearly eight o'clock in the evening when the train pulled into cow town. The platform was full of anxious families, each waiting for the first glimpse of their loved ones.

Doris was almost ready to pass out with the emotion of seeing LW again. When he stepped off the train, not one member of his family recognized him. Dressed in his navy blues, LW walked straight toward his mother. When he was twenty feet away, his mother and Doris recognized him, though he could tell that his father and uncles were still unaware of his location. Both Doris and his mother were crying when he walked into their arms.

Doris could not believe her eyes. The man who walked so confidently toward her looked like the lead character from some Hollywood movie. The change in the boy she loved was breathtaking. On the ride home, LW sat in the back seat with Doris. He leaned over and gave her a quick kiss the cheek. He cleared his throat and said, "I am headed for flight school in Florida. I have three weeks before I have to leave." His mother looked at her husband and smiled. Three weeks was not long, but beggars could not be choosers.

That night, while sitting on his porch with Doris, he told her his plans.

"I don't want to wait to get married. I want to do it while I am on leave."

Doris was shocked. Getting married was every girl's dream, but to be asked to do so on such short notice was unheard of. She said as much to LW. His answer was predictable but compelling, one that had been used for time immemorial.

"But this is different. This is wartime. You never know if I'll be required to give my life for the cause. I don't want to wait. I need to know that you're mine. It's the only way I can keep my mind on staying alive. I know your mother would never approve. So we will just do it and tell her when the time is right; then she will have to accept it. " When he finished speaking, he held both her hands and looked longingly into her eyes.

Doris was confused. She loved him and wanted to spend the rest of her life with him, but her mother would be extremely disappointed. She wanted a big wedding for her daughter. Finally, as so often occurs with the female of our species, she simply could not deny him.

Shyly, she said, "Yes, I will."

LW jumped up and down. "When?"

"Whenever you want."

"Okay, I'll find the best way to do it. But we have to keep it a secret. I mean it, we won't tell anyone." She smiled and gave him a quick kiss. After a brief good-bye, LW walked her home. They proceeded in silence, both lost in their own thoughts. Finally, when they were standing in front of her house, LW looked down and asked, "Are you sure?"

"Yes, I am," Doris said with a smile.

"Well then this is the last time we say good-bye as boyfriend and girlfriend."

"I guess so." LW gave her a quick hug.

Unbeknownst to the two star-struck lovers, a watchful set of eyes had been observing them. Doris's mother, certain that a hug was all that was going to transpire and that the foul boy had no further expectations, turned on her husband and growled, "I don't care how much you like his parents. That boy is no good."

"Now, dear, LW has done nothing wrong. He has been gone almost a year and they appear to still be in love. Maybe you should let things play out."

"I'll let them play out, all right."

Doris came in and gave both her parents a kiss and a hug, a strange, lingering hug that put her mother on edge.

"Good night, Mom and Dad." Her father looked up smiled. Her mother just glared. Doris saw the look in her mother's eyes and felt a twinge of regret. She quickly exited the room before her eyes betrayed her great secret.

Her mother watched her go and turned to her husband. "There's something going on. She's up to something."

"Now what has she done to deserve suspicion?" her husband wanted to know. His wife said nothing, but she continued to stare toward her daughter's room.

The morning arrived with an awe-inspiring sunrise. LW had spent a sleepless night plotting out his wedding. He first confirmed that he could borrow the car for the afternoon and then walked down to Doris's house to invite her on a lunch date later that day. That done, he went about making his mother happy in any way he could. He headed to Doris's house at about one o'clock that afternoon. Her mother was sitting in the window, watching as they drove away. Doris was smiling but had tears in her eyes. He looked at her and felt a pain in his heart. Was she having second thoughts? He felt panic as the thought took hold.

"If you don't want to do this, I'll understand." He held his breath as he awaited her reply.

She held his whole world in the palm of her hand. She looked at him, and tears washed the sides of her face.

"I have never wanted anything so badly in all my life. It's just that my mother wanted me to have a big wedding. I feel like I am letting her down."

He slipped his arm around her, and she slid over beside him. "Your mother would never give us her blessing. Besides, we are going to keep it secret. Later on we can have a big wedding."

She smiled as they pulled onto the highway. They found the courthouse, and an hour later they walked out as man and wife. On the way back to her house, LW turned onto his street and pulled up into the driveway. "Come on, this will only take a minute."

She had no idea what he was up to but followed him into the living room. His mother and father were listening to the radio and smiled as they entered the room. His father stood up and said, "We just got word that Henry is on his way here. He should be on the eight o'clock train tomorrow morning."

"That's great news, Dad. I can't wait to see him. By the way, Doris and I got married today." His mother just sat there. Doris was shocked, and his father thought he had not heard correctly.

"I am sorry, son, what did you say?"

"I said I can't wait to see him."

"No, after that."

"Oh, I said we got married."

His father fell back into his chair. Doris was the first to react.

"What happened to keeping it secret?"

"I am sorry. It's just that you're my wife now and I don't care who knows it."

She was so stunned that she just stood and stared at the three of them. Finally, after a few moments of stunned silence, LW's mother stood up and reached for Doris.

"I have a daughter! I'm glad it is you." They both broke down in tears. His father reached out a hand.

"I guess congratulations are in order. Her mother seems to have taken this pretty well, it seems."

Doris hung her head while LW cleared his throat. "They don't know yet. We wanted to tell you first."

"LW, that's not the way it should be done!" his mother exclaimed.

His father gave him a stern look and grabbed the car keys. "Let's go."

His father did not say a word as they drove the short distance to Doris's house. Though he did not talk to his son, he was watching him and noted the stubborn look and the set jaw. He was proud and amused at the same time. He could see the boy he raised and knew, as well as the man LW had become. He asked LW to wait in the car and headed for the door. He felt his son standing beside him and felt relief wash over him. LW had indeed become a man.

"Dad, I'll tell them. It's my place, not yours."

"Whatever you want, son."

Doris's father opened the door and was visibly shaken when he saw the expressions written on the faces of his guests. "Mary Ellen, come here. You boys better come in." He sat down heavily and awaited the news he knew was coming.

"Well, is my daughter in trouble?" Doris's mother asked.

"Depends on how you look at it," LW's father said quietly. LW looked her mother in the eyes and was surprised at the animosity evident there. The anger was flowing like liquid hatred, threatening to engulf him.

"What have you done to my little girl?" she asked, her voice cutting through the air.

"Doris is now my wife," LW said defiantly.

"Nothing inappropriate has occurred," LW's father said quickly.

Doris's father practically jumped up and shook their hands. He seemed to find new life, and it was apparent that he had been braced for the worst.

This caught LW by surprise. He had expected a fist or shouting or something. He looked over at Doris's mother and received the same icy stare as before. She simply asked where they would live. Once assured that it would not be with them, she turned and walked out of the room.

"Well now, LW, how do expect to support my daughter?"

"Once I am through my first month of flight school, I can apply for married quarters. My salary should cover everything we need."

Her father's face grew stern. "You know you should have asked for my blessing first."

LW dropped his eyes in shame. "Yes, sir, I know it."

"That's why I brought him over, and I came myself to apologize," LW Sr. added.

"Why did you not wait for a big wedding?"

"I love her and I want to be with her forever. And …"

"And what?" Now her father grew nervous again.

"And we didn't think her mother would ever give us her blessing and she would turn Doris's wedding into a nightmare."

His new father-in-law had to admit the boy was right. It would have been a terrible ordeal for everyone. At least this way he would not bear the brunt of her anger by having to give his consent. The couple had dated for an acceptable period of time, and now his wife's anger would almost solely be placed on the boy. The bright side of the crisis far outweighed the bad.

"Well, I expect it's meant to be. She will probably want to come over and pack her things." Just as he got the words out, a suitcase came flying over the couch and crash-landed at LW's feet.

"She's not coming back here tonight. Tell her she can get the rest of her stuff tomorrow while I'm shopping." Doris's mother turned and, without another sound, walked into the kitchen.

"I guess she doesn't need to come and get her stuff after all," her father remarked.

"LW, why don't you take that suitcase out to the car," LW Sr. said. The two men watched LW walk out the door. His father eyed the other man for a moment and then asked, "You think she will be all right?"

"Hell no! But she will have to get used to it." LW Sr. quietly thanked his lucky stars that he wasn't married to her.

When they arrived home, they found the two women making dinner in the kitchen. LW's mother looked up and smiled while Doris went over and hugged LW. It was an awkward evening for all four of them. For Doris, the moment they said good night was the most embarrassing of her life. LW did little to ease her situation. "Good night, Dad. We're going to bed. I would say sleep, but I doubt we'll sleep much." LW laughed, and Doris slapped him in the arm.

The following morning, Henry arrived and was greeted by his entire family. While he was hugging his mother, he saw an officer approach and snapped to attention. It was only after the smirking officer returned his salute that he recognized his cousin. "You have to be kidding me. They really made you an officer?"

"They know greatness when they see it."

"Well, officer or not, I'll always be your superior." With a laugh, the two cousins embraced. Henry spent the next week just hanging out with Doris and LW. He was amazed at the love that was apparent between the two newlyweds. LW, for his part, was stunned at how much he felt for Doris. He knew that he had never been this happy. He ached for her every moment of the day. They spent time between his parents' house and hers. Her father had evidently won the battle and persuaded her mother to accept the inevitable. His parents were constantly inviting their new in-laws over, and LW was getting a large dose of his mother-in-law. To his credit, he took it all in stride, remaining polite and respectful. Doris could not have been more disappointed in her mother or more proud of her new husband.

One morning, Henry and LW were going squirrel hunting, and Doris would not be left behind. They took his dad's car down to the river and suited up. "Here, Doris, put this vest on," LW said with a smile.

"Now, LW, she doesn't need to wear that."

"She wants the full experience doesn't she," LW replied with a smile.

Doris was not about to be shown up. "You bet I do, and I'll probably show you boys a thing or two while I'm at it," she said sharply.

Both Henry and LW got a laugh out of this. Henry went up the river, and LW and Doris began walking down it. It wasn't long before LW spotted a squirrel and quickly dropped it. He picked it up and continued on his way.

"Do you want a shot, Doris?" he asked innocently.

"No, I don't want to embarrass you."

He raised the rifle for another shot, and Doris walked up and kissed his ear. The bullet flew harmlessly through the air. LW turned in anger, only to see her smiling face. He smiled and threw his arms around her. They embraced in lover's desperation as only those who have found their true love and are soon to be separated can. As they looked into each other's eyes, they were lost to time. LW felt the love in his heart swell to match the current of the flowing river beside which they lay. "I love you more than anything in the world," he said passionately. She smiled as tears began to roll down her face. He gently kissed them away. The sound of squirrels playing in the trees and a rifle shot echoing down the river finally brought his mind back to the original purpose of the trip. He resumed the hunt and bagged three squirrels on his next three shots. As he went to pick up the last one, he noticed that it was still breathing. A thought crossed his mind and he quickly moved to put it into the pouch on the back of Doris's vest.

"What are you doing."

"My pouch is full. I need to use yours."

"Okay. It won't get blood on me, will it?"

"You'll be fine."

They began walking back to the car, holding hands. LW made sure that he was on her right, holding her right hand with his left.

"So how long will you be gone?"

"I have about six weeks of school and then I will send for you."

"That's a long time," she replied.

"It is a long time."

"Why can't ..." Suddenly, she went stiff. And then she started screaming, trying desperately to break his grip on her hand. LW was boiling with laughter. The unconscious squirrel in her vest pouch had finally awoke.

"Get it off! Get it off! Get it off!" she screamed.

"Get what off? I can't help you if you don't tell me what's wrong."

"It's alive! It's alive! Get it off!" She was desperate now. He could not resist her any longer and he released his hold. She immediately began running in circles, screaming and batting at her back. LW finally caught her and removed the squirrel. She sat down and began to cry. This made him feel a little remorse, and he sat to comfort her.

"I'm sorry. It was really just nerves. It was dead."

"You did that on purpose."

"I did not. How was I supposed to know that it wasn't dead?"

"I don't know, but you did."

LW was still smiling when they met Henry back at the car. When Henry heard the story, he laughed uncontrollably even though he felt sorry for her.

"Laugh all you want, Henry. I'll get back at you." Henry sobered a little. Threats from a woman were something new to him.

LW dropped Doris off at his house and he then went to take Henry home.

"LW, that was a dirty thing to do. Do you think it worked?"

"Yep, I think her hunting days are over." They both shared a laugh and then stopped for a beer. This was LW's final night before shipping off to Florida. He loved his cousin, but he was in a hurry to get back to his wife. Henry was staring into his glass and not saying much.

"I'm going to get back to Doris."

"You know, they're very good."

"Who's very good?"

"They use their aircraft as forward artillery."

"What are you talking about, Henry?"

"The Germans; they are going to be tough."

"Well, if you army boys can't handle them, then I guess the navy will have to win this war, too."

Henry started laughing and slapped LW on the back. "I'll see ya later, LW."

"You take care of yourself out there, Henry. Don't do anything stupid." LW left Henry sitting at the bar and made his way home. He was worried about Henry. If Henry was scared, then there was something to be scared of.

LW and Doris spent a sleepless night making plans for the future and enjoying their time together. Way too early, the morning light began penetrating their sanctuary of darkness. Soon the smell of coffee and bacon filled the room. LW arose and headed for the shower while Doris slipped into her nightgown and headed for the kitchen. Tears still glistened on her cheeks as she moved up beside her mother-in-law and began helping. LW's mother gave her a huge hug, and both women shared a good cry.

"It's hard to let go, isn't it?"

"I thought it would be easier this time, but it's not," Doris replied.

"That bacon cooks any longer and we can make shoes out of it," LW Sr. said as he sat down in his chair. "You women ought to be thinking more of that boy than yourselves. What do you think it does to him to have to leave two crying females behind?"

Neither woman said a word, but both continued to cry. They did much better at the train station than they had before. But as LW stood waving out the door as the train pulled away, even his father could not fight back the tears. Henry sat on the hood of his car, watching as the train roared by. He didn't even take the time to wipe the tears that ran freely down his cheeks.

Chapter Seven

LW had never seen so much water. Not that he hadn't seen the ocean before, but this water spread out in every direction. Even the land was inundated with it. After getting settled in, he went down to the beach and wrote letters to Doris and his mother. Training started the very next day, with a brisk run on the beach. After the workout, the men went back to the classroom and studied aeronautics. LW found the school work a little boring, but he made it through the first three weeks without too much trouble. During that time, they also learned basic flight training and survival techniques.

The day finally came when LW took his first flight in an airplane. It was a two-seater training plane, with LW in the front and a flight instructor in the back. He felt his excitement grow as the plane roared down the runway. The little plane bounced twice and soared skyward. The instructor could tell how much LW was enjoying it, and he smiled as they headed out to sea.

As the land gave way to the massive expanse of the sea, LW held his breath. He had never seen anything so beautiful or so big. The instructor told him to take the stick. LW took control of the plane and flew straight for a while before putting the craft into a gentle turn and then a small dive. He was now headed back for land and could see the beach some five thousand feet below. Putting the plane into a much steeper dive, LW could barely make out the voice of his instructor gently offering advice. He pulled the craft up and then banked hard to the left, climbed, banked hard to the right, and dove. He could hear his instructor screaming encouragement. LW needed no encouragement; this was incredible. He could not believe that he was getting paid for this. His instructor had to threaten him before LW would relinquish control. When they landed, LW was all smiles. His instructor slapped him on the back and talked about the dives they had made.

Flight training slowly took over his life. Every morning, he spent four hours in a classroom, and every afternoon was spent in an airplane. He made his first solo flight three weeks later. He was to fly thirty miles up the coast before returning and practice touch and goes. His takeoff was almost perfect, one wheel and then the other coming of the tarmac. His plane lifted up, and he climbed to a thousand feet and headed north. Keeping the beach just off his right wing, he felt as if he was born for this. Way too soon, the thirty mile limit was reached, and he made a slow turn and put the beach on his left wing. When he saw the airport, he dove to five hundred feet and began to circle the runway. With each circle, he lost one hundred feet of altitude. Listening carefully to the control tower, he moved quickly into his landing pattern and let his wheels touch the ground ever so gently. He felt the impact as the plane touched down, and then he hit the throttle wide open and gained altitude. This was the only time LW felt even a hint of anxiety. He could sense the plane struggling to rise above the pull of the earth, and he willed it to succeed. Finally, the craft began streaking skyward, and LW took a breath. The runway was falling rapidly behind him, and he could just make out another plane touching down behind him. His radio cracked with information on speed, angle, and altitude. Although everyone had been briefed before, LW was still taken aback by the sight of all the planes flying in circles above the airfield. As he watched the twenty-odd airplanes circling, a frantic voice came over the radio.

"Full throttle. Full throttle! Pull up!" LW could see a flash on the ground and then black smoke as rescue workers moved in. The entire wing was ordered into a holding pattern while they cleared the runway. It would not be the last time he would see a plane crash, nor would it be the last time he would watch helplessly as one of his own went down.

LW had stood at attention while his flight instructor had chewed him out. It was against regulations for a trainee to get married, so LW could have rightly been dismissed from the air wing and spent the remainder of the war on board a ship. As it happened, his instructor had also become his friend. So LW sat through a ten-minute lecture and then was told to go to housing and put in his request. Two weeks later, he was informed that a housing unit nearing completion would be his new home. The unit would be ready in one week. LW bought a train ticket and put it, along with some money, in a envelope and sent it home to Doris. The ticket was for two weeks from Saturday and he could not wait. That weekend, LW was able to take possession of his new home. He went to town and bought a table, chairs, groceries, and other small items. He decided to leave the bigger purchases to his new bride. As the week progressed, LW was having a harder time concentrating. He was knocked flat during one of his numerous boxing matches.

Finally the day came, and LW was standing at the train platform with flowers in hand. When Doris stepped off the train, he could hardly contain his joy. She ran into his arms, and they embraced. They stood there, holding on to each other. Finally, people began to stare, and reluctantly they stepped back and caught their breath.

"You look great, Doris. I have missed you so much."

"It took forever to get here."

They took a cab back to the base, and Doris smiled when she saw their first house. She walked up to the door, and LW caught her arm.

"Oh no you don't. I'm going to carry you across the doorway." With that, he lifted her up and carried her into the house. She looked at the small kitchen that doubled as a dining room and the bare living room. Her eyes went to the bedroom, but she had no intentions of being lured in there just yet.

"We need furniture."

"I know. I bought just the basics. I thought it was better if we shopped together. We have enough food to last until Monday. But I borrowed a friend's car so we could go shopping this afternoon."

"That's wonderful, LW, but can we afford a couch and bedroom furniture?"

"We should be fine. I have a hundred and fifty dollars saved up, and I get paid next week." This time she didn't say anything but was silently thankful that LW had lived so frugally. Another sign of his love for her.

"I have five hundred dollars in my purse," she said with a grin.

"How did you get so much?"

"Our parents' wedding gifts, and my own savings." It was LW's turn to smile. Laughing the two finally inspected the bedroom.

Doris and LW spent the rest of the afternoon shopping and finished the day with a nice dinner in town. They went to church the next day and attended a cookout over at one of the other married men's house. The following morning, LW went off to work like any other normal newlywed. The only difference was that his work consisted of flying airplanes at breakneck speeds. Doris was kept busy by the deliveries that began showing up around eight o'clock. The couch, love seat, coffee table, and a chair were the first to arrive. This was followed by their bedroom set and then finally the truck with the rugs, towels, dinnerware, lamps, and radio. She had managed to spend almost half their money, and she had one thing left to shop for. She walked down to the base grocery store and placed her order. By the time LW got home, she had received their groceries and cooked him ham and potatoes. They sat on the porch that night, listening to the radio and eating apple pie. A news flash came on about great battles raging around the world. They snuggled closer together and held on tight.

*****

Henry was damn tired: tired of being on a boat, tired of the ocean, but most of all, tired of being shot at every night. Those U-boats were not as bad as the navy had told them; they were worse. It seemed like every night, two or three ships were lost. At last, they were told where they were headed: Africa. The good news was they were very close. The bad news was that Rommel was waiting for them. The final fighting would be done in Europe, which Henry assumed would put them back on boats again. They would be docking tomorrow, and nobody seemed to be able to tell them if they would be unloading under fire. They didn't know which side the French would be on—typical of the French. Henry's three tanks were probably rotting in the hold. The best case scenario was that they would work fine until deep in combat. Then something that they didn't check would snap and leave them at the mercy of the Germans.

With a final scan of the dark water, assured that no U-boat was bearing down on them at the moment, Henry went below deck and sought out his bunk. His sleep was broken by alarms and screams, men running, and water, lots of water. Henry fought to climb the stairwell. Water was already pouring through the hatch. Suddenly, an explosion sent him flying across the deck. He saw a huge, dark shape moving silently forward. Henry jumped into the waiting sea below. It was just before he hit the water that Henry awoke from his dream.

He shook his head, trying to clear his thoughts. Something didn't feel right. Henry went to the bathroom and took a quick shower. Afterward, as he made his way up the decks, he noticed how deserted the ship was. Sunlight hit him like a hammer. Before him lay a large bay, packed full of ships. Men and equipment flowed in every conceivable direction. Just beyond the docks, he could make out the town, covered in thick black smoke. Aircraft of all sizes zipped in and out of view. He watched as the vessel in front of his disgorged equipment and men. He realized that his ship was next in line and went below to grab his belongings. His crew was waiting at their tanks, carefully avoiding the sailors who scurried and crawled over the stored machines. Suddenly, the hatch above opened, and he divided his men into groups to assist with the unloading. Breakfast was served on the dock as they performed quick checks on the tanks. They seemed to be okay, but until they were able to check them in the field, he would not feel safe.

It took them an hour to get clear of the harbor and drive into town. Henry was far too worried about navigating the small streets than he was about observing the local scenery. Lunch was served on the road above town. Henry ate while walking from tank to tank. Traffic had come to a dead stop, and Henry was taking the time to do a systems check and run some drills. As he did this, a Jeep roared up and a small officer jumped out with orders for Henry. A large force of French men were entrenched up the road, and Henry's men were to proceed there immediately and engage. Henry looked at the officer like he was crazy. They didn't have the fuel to go racing forward and fight a battle, not to mention the fact that they had no main gun ammo. The officer had no idea how Henry was to accomplish this, only that he was. Henry cussed and then ordered his tanks to move off the side of the road and then proceed forward. He watched as the other tanks in his group followed his orders. Then he turned and asked the small officer where his captain was. The officer just shook his head and ran off. Henry had not seen any of his commanders since the morning briefing. The scenario was playing out just as Henry had feared. He was going into combat without preparation and without guidance.

Henry passed some fuel trucks and got them to pull over and fuel all sixteen tanks. To his surprise, several supply trucks pulled up and unloaded ammo. He was shocked to see them quickly stack the rounds on the ground and then race off toward the fighting.

Five miles farther up the road, they saw their first casualties. Burning vehicles and smoldering craters told them that they were now in range of enemy guns. The air was pierced by the screams of incoming rounds. The road exploded and rained destruction down on the dead. Henry had his tanks about fifty yards off the road. Had they been on it, they would now be smoking hulks. He quickly ordered his three tanks into battle formation and watched as the other team leaders followed suit. The twelve tanks spread out and began rumbling forward toward a low, tree-covered hill. Artillery shells fell behind them, He realized that the enemy could hear his tanks but could not see them. He ordered his tanks to increase their speed and load their main guns.

He glanced up and saw an aircraft banking and diving toward them. He sighed with relief. The plane should easily be able to take out the enemy gun emplacements. To his horror, the plane continued to dive straight at them, and then a tank on the far end of the line exploded in a ball of flame. His loader wanted to know what had happened, and Henry had to scream to be heard.

"One of our tanks just got taken out by an airplane."

"Why is the plane shooting at us?" asked the confused gunner.

"Probably because it's German."

"Oh God." The boy issued a silent prayer. Things then went from bad to worse. Their driver had been listening to the conversation and decided the closer they were to the enemy, the safer they were. He was now driving like a mad man. All Henry could do was watch as the plane banked and began the slow dive again.

As they crested the hill, they found the other side crawling with men and equipment. Henry slammed the hatch shut and aimed the main gun. If the loader needed any more info on whose side they were on, Henry answered him. He sighted two half tracks turning to engage him. He swung the gun on the first and turned it into a twisted heap of burning metal. "Load. Load," Henry called out. He watched as his target exploded; one of his other tanks had taken it out. Henry opened the hatch and began working the machine gun, spraying bullets through the confused enemy horde. The appearance of so many American tanks had broken the spirit of the defenders. Now the tanks were hosing them down with hot lead. Their formations wavered and then broke into a panicked retreat. Henry spotted the artillery a few hundred feet away. They were watching in frustration, unable to fire for fear of hitting their own people. Henry headed straight for them, sighting the closest one, and cut its crew to shreds. Moving from one to the other, the three tanks wiped out the guns in a matter of minutes.

They sat among the burning carnage and looked back along their path of destruction. Henry counted seven tanks still fighting, mopping up the remaining enemy pockets. As Henry watched, one of the tanks exploded, then another. Alarmed, he looked skyward for the offending threat. To his amazement, four enemy tanks materialized between him and the rest of the Americans. It was the Americans' turn to be caught off guard. Confusion now reigned. The four tanks were so bent on destruction that they did not even see Henry's three tanks sitting on the side of the hill. Just like target practice, all three tanks fired on the same objective. The last tank to the left exploded, its turret going up like a rocket, a smoke trail marking its path. The second tank died in much the same way, while the remaining two continued to kill. Henry sighted the third enemy tank and watched it shudder with the impact. Henry fired a second volley and was rewarded with black smoke issuing from the engine. The fourth tank died in a similar fashion; its crew poured from the front hatch. Just when he thought they would get clear, the tank was hit again and exploded. Henry watched as a burning American tank slowly crawled by the now burning fourth enemy tank.

The last act of its crew had been to kill their enemy. His three tanks still sat side by side among the destroyed gun batteries.

It fell eerily silent, though the sounds of war could be heard in the distance. Henry realized that the only survivors of the carnage were his three tanks. Henry climbed out of his vehicle and vomited. The smell of burning flesh and fuel hung thick in the air. Their first day—really their first hour—of war had been a bad one. He knew their survival had more to do with luck than skill. Not wanting to tempt fate, Henry ordered his men to enter the tree line on the hill they first crossed and to spread out. Having already seen the destructive power of aircraft, he cut down branches and tried to use them to conceal the tanks. Having taken out the road block and cleared the gun nests, they had no idea what to do next. Henry began gathering the dead tankers, or what he could find of them. Most of the vehicles were too hot to touch. He did find six wounded prisoners. They seemed to be a mix of German, French, and natives. The Americans gave them what medical help they could and then gathered up the weapons that lay scattered about. Henry noticed a young driver walking over to him. "What's wrong, Scott?" he asked.

"I was just wondering why we're helping these guys."

"You mean besides because it's the right thing to do?"

"Yes besides that," he said with anger in his voice.

"Well, what if the Germans show up before our guys?"

Scott hadn't thought about that. "I see. If we treat them badly then they will treat us badly. That's smart." Henry didn't say a word. He just turned and walked down to the road. They found fourteen dead and three wounded Americans among the wreckage. Henry sat down on a fallen tree and began writing down everything he could remember. He could still hear the rumble of guns in the distance.

After a couple of hours, trucks began rolling down the highway towards him. Henry breathed a sigh of relief when he saw the white star on their sides. Nearly out of gas, with only seven rounds between them, his own tanks would have made a sorry fight if the Germans had reached them first. He ordered his tanks to remove their camouflage. He did not want to be mistaken for Germans. As his tanks roared to life and rolled forward, the convey came to a halt. After a moment, the trucks started forward again, this time a little more cautiously. Henry climbed down and walked out to the road to meet them. As they rolled up, infantry poured out of the trucks and began checking the burning vehicles. "The bad guys are over the hill," Henry said, clearly tired.

"You guys all that are left?" the driver asked in awe.

"We moved the wounded over into that depression. Got some prisoners there, too," Henry said with little emotion. Now he had their attention. They walked over to inspect the prisoners. To Henry's relief, a medic was among them. Then a Jeep pulled up and a captain got out. Henry snapped to attention. "Sir."

"Those tanks belong to you?"

"Yes, sir."

"What happened?"

Henry explained in detail, leading the captain over to view the battlefield. When he was finished, the captain whistled. "Hell of a fight. Well, my orders were to find you guys and hold a perimeter for the night. Think we'll move up that ridge where the guns are. You boys get fuelled up and move over to the other side of that second hill."

"Yes, sir." Henry snapped a salute and moved toward his tanks. They would drive back over the hill they had just vacated. He prepared for his first night in Africa. *Better than being on a ship*, he thought. *At least here I can fight back.*

*****

Billy was sick of Hawaii. They had been here for six weeks, and he was long out of things to do. The navy owned this island, and as far as he was concerned, they could have it. So when the news came about their victory at Midway, he began to get jittery. From all reports, it had been a massive blow to the Japanese offensive capabilities. His commander had been very excited about it and said the carrier ratio was tilting their way. He had no idea what that meant and didn't care. The important part of it was that Japan was on the defensive side, and he had a pretty good idea of what or whom they were going to be fighting off.

Billy was learning to hate the islands. Their beauty hid the death and carnage that awaited just beyond the tree lines. He never wanted to see another island again, though he had a feeling he would be seeing more of them before this war was over.

*****

Graduation finally came, and Doris was extremely excited. LW was to spend an additional twelve weeks on the base, learning advanced combat training. That meant that they could stay in their little house for another three months. She was sad that half his group was leaving for other schools. Only half had qualified for fighters. But they still had friends who would be here, and both her parents and LW's were coming out for the ceremony. She had seen LW fly over their house on many occasions and even got to watch from the runway once.

Together they had put in a vegetable garden, and she had planted some flowers along the sidewalk. LW had bought a grill, and they often cooked out. She was unbelievably happy. That evening after dinner, they went for a walk down the beach. Hand in hand, they walked in and out of the surf, finding seashells or seeing fish. There was always something. They listened to the roar of the waves and the sound of gulls. This matched her dreams in every way.

LW walked around in a daze, lost in his love for his wife. Walking on the beach with her was like scoring the game-winning point. The poets who he had always made fun of were in the end, right; love was the most incredible thing he had ever felt. And each day, his love for Doris seemed to grow. He could no longer imagine life without her. He had not really wanted a garden, but she had insisted. Now he knew he would put one in every year and it would remind him of this time. His world was perfect—his job, his home, all perfect. But now a dark cloud was descending on them. His mother-in-law would arrive tomorrow. He secretly hated her but would never admit that to Doris. The lady picked on him and gave him dirty looks. But he knew that for Doris he could endure it forever. He could not wait to show his dad their house and the airplanes. Most of all, he could not wait to show his mother their little garden. He drank in the moment, trying to forget about tomorrow. Doris had found a wad of sea weed and picked that moment to wrap it around LW's head. He howled and then chased her out into the surf, where they embraced and then splashed at each other. Later that evening, they sat on a towel, listening to the ocean and watching the stars.

"Hard to believe that there is a war being fought," LW said.

"Yes it is," she said quietly.

"When I finally go out on patrol, and I am staring up at the stars, I will remember this moment."

"As long as you remember that it was me you were with."

"Now why would I forget something like that?" he asked, alarmed.

"I know all about those Asian girls. So exotic, so exciting. You better not forget me," she said with a serious look on her face.

He laughed. "Now I wouldn't say that I would totally forget, but maybe a momentary lapse in memory." She punched him in the arm, and he picked her up and carried her into the surf.

The next morning, they were waiting at the station when their parents pulled up. "Here we go," LW said. Doris thought about punching him again. His father wrapped him in a bear hug, while his mother cried and hugged Doris. Her father embraced her tightly and shook LW's hand. He then stepped back and made room for her mother. She gave Doris a quick hug and then looked at the sky. "Is it always this humid? I hear that there are no winters in Florida."

LW smiled. "No, ma'am, it's usually much more humid than this, and just this winter we had a foot of snow." Doris's father suddenly began to choke, and LW Sr. laughed out loud.

They loaded up in a car LW managed to borrow and headed out to the base. LW Sr. managed to slam his fingers in the car door and then proceeded to cuss them out. When they got their first view of the beach, LW heard his mother catch her breath. "Wow, it's beautiful," was all she could say.

At the gate, LW handed the marine his paperwork and they proceeded into the base. LW purposely took the long way home, driving by the parked fighters, wings glistening in the sun. Just as they reached their turn, a fighter roared off the runway and flew directly over their car. Doris's mother was the first to break the silence.

"How can you live with all this noise?"

"Mom, the planes usually only fly during the day. Besides, it's reassuring knowing that all these planes are here. And after a few days, the noise just seems natural," Doris said with a forced smile.

"Will we get to see you fly?" LW's mother asked sweetly.

"I have a final flight scheduled for eight tomorrow morning. You can't get to the runway, but you should be able to see me from the front yard."

That night, the men sat on the front porch, drinking beer and listening to the radio. The news flashes reported battles from all over the world. There were great air and sea battles in the Pacific and air battles over Europe. The Russian front was still holding, and in North Africa, the Allies were driving forward. "This is truly a world war," LW said grimly. They listened to news of the great carrier battle off a tiny island called Midway. There were reports of four Japanese carriers sunk. The men slapped each other on the back an made predictions about how fast the Japanese would fold. The next morning, they all gathered on the lawn and watched as LW flew over and shook his wings so that they would know which plane was his. He flew over the house and then banked high and disappeared into the distance. His mother held her breath and silently prayed for her son's safety. After much discussion, it was decided that they would let Doris show them the beach. LW Sr. was amazed at the clarity of the water and soon found himself learning to body surf. The women sat under umbrellas and watched the men swim and tumble in the water. Doris watched as LW's father came running out of the water, screaming and clawing at his face. It took about five minutes for him to calm down enough to explain what had happened. As he surfaced, a Portuguese Man o' War had washed over him. The jellyfish had ended up sitting on his head, and its tentacles had wrapped around him from head to toe. After ten minutes, he was having trouble standing and was short of breath. Doris could not hide her amusement at the incredible language that was issuing from the mouth of the victim.

When LW got home that night, he found his father covered in cooking grease, with a glass of whiskey in one hand and a pipe in the other.

"What wrong with you?" LW asked.

"I was attacked by a jellyfish," his father replied with as much dignity as he could muster.

"Jellyfish don't attack people."

"This one did."

"What kind of jellyfish was it?"

"A big purple one. Must have been twenty feet long."

"You're drunk."

"Damn right I am."

"It was pretty bad, LW. He was wrapped from head to foot," Doris's father said, coming to the defense of his friend. LW went in and found Doris, her mother, and his mother sitting in the kitchen. They were putting the final touches on a casserole.

"So I guess Dad has been playing up his injury?"

"It was horrible. He was covered in stingers," his mother replied.

"Well he sure isn't feeling it now."

"That's okay. He was in terrible pain. I told him to drink as much as possible," his mother said sweetly.

"That's like letting a pig loose in a vegetable garden," LW said sourly.

"You hush and go clean up for dinner," Doris said, getting angry. His mother was silently pleased with her daughter-in-law. She had kept her peace an appropriate time and then firmly put LW in his place. There was a lot of potential there. With time and her help, Doris would make a powerful ally against her two men.

Doris's mother was not happy at all. She had stayed away from her house far longer than she liked and was ready to leave. She didn't care one cent for her son-in-law and less for his father, although she liked his mother. How in the world LW's mother put up with the two of them was far beyond her understanding.

Doris carried two plates out to the men and laughed when LW Sr. fell out of his chair.

LW stood at attention as his wings were pinned on. He could see his parents and his wife. His mother and Doris had tears running down their cheeks, and even his father seemed to be wiping his eyes. He was now a naval aviator; more so, he was a fighter pilot. His chest swelled with the weight of the gold wings hanging off his uniform. It would not be long now until he could prove himself against the Japanese. After the ceremony, the families were allowed to walk around the assembled aircraft. LW proudly showed off his knowledge and eagerly explained the different levers and gauges to his captive audience. Doris smiled sweetly and listened to LW explaining the complicated craft. Though she only understood about half of what was said, she gave her husband her full attention. This was his day, and she could not have been prouder. His father put his arm around his son and smiled.

"I am very proud of you, son. It took a lot to get this far."

"Thanks, Dad. I still have a long way to go."

"I can't believe you can actually fly this thing," his mother-in-law said.

"I've spent a lot of time learning how," he replied

"As long as you don't ever take my daughter flying, then I couldn't care less."

LW bit down on his lip and walked over to his mother. She stood watching him, tears still welling up in her eyes.

"What's wrong, Mom?"

"I am just so proud of you. No matter how big you get, you will always be my little boy."

"Mother, I am not little anymore. I am a married naval pilot." LW began to blush. His mother didn't say anything. She just smiled and kissed him on the cheek.

Later that evening, as they sat having dinner, LW received a telegram from Harold's father. He got up and slowly walked outside. Doris got worried and followed him. After a few moments, Doris saw the tears in her husband's eyes. She threw her arms around him and squeezed. She had no idea what the letter contained, but she knew that it was not good news.

LW looked up and said in a strained voice, "Harold's plane went down over the Rockies. There were no survivors."

Doris felt her stomach turn. Harold was her first boyfriend, and one of LW's best friends. "What happened?" she asked.

"I don't know, only that the weather was bad."

Their parents came out and shared their children's grief. Each had known Harold to some extent, and the loss troubled them greatly. The war had just become much, much more personal. The mood in the little house would remain subdued, each lost in his or her own thoughts.

LW was sinking in a pool of despair and sorrow. His shock at the loss of a friend and the cold, hard reality of his own mortality brought down a cloak of depression. The war was no longer a faraway surreal event. Now it was a living, breathing demon that could at any time reach out an icy claw and claim a life that was precious to him. The fight had become personal.

Few words were spoken at the train station as LW and Doris said good-bye to their parents. Afterward, LW threw himself into his training, trying to keep his mind occupied. Every night he said a silent prayer for the safety of his cousins. His three months flew by, and LW surpassed all expectations and finished first in his class. He was informed that his orders would arrive within a few days and he should start packing. Doris was sad to leave their little house; she would always treasure their time there. Like a good trooper, she kept her pain to herself and was packed up in three days' time. Despite the emotions he was going through, LW felt proud at the way Doris stood up to the move. He received his orders the very next morning. He was to report for duty in San Diego in three weeks.

That night, they decided to eat dinner on the beach. They watched as a destroyer slowly sailed back and forth. LW was fascinated with the ship's maneuvering. It would suddenly speed up and then come to a dead stop. After about five minutes, the vessel drew relatively close to the beach and began tossing things off the stern. LW and Doris watched in silence, unaware of the purpose of such a thing. After a moment, water erupted behind the ship, again and again. LW stood up and put a hand over his eyes, trying to make out the scene in better detail.

"I think they found a sub," he said.

"What are you talking about?" she asked, perplexed.

"A sub. They're trying to kill a sub."

"Why would they do that?" she asked, more confused than ever.

"Because it's probably German."

"You mean from Germany?"

"Yes, from Germany." The destroyer was now turning around and heading back over the area of the explosions. They watched until darkness veiled the predator from view. They felt like they had had an out of body experience, shocked by the war's sudden appearance in their backyard. As they walked back to their house, they could hear muffled roars as the battle resumed. That night, they held each other tight, each trying to come to terms with the dark and hazy future.

Chapter Eight

Henry could not believe his luck. After fighting his way across Africa and managing somehow to keep his tanks intact, he now found himself about to come face-to-face with the desert fox. For his honorable service and surviving his countless engagements, Henry had been promoted. For keeping his other two tanks from being blown up, they had given him command of more tanks and honored him by allowing his tanks to take up the extreme forward position in the current engagement. Henry was proud of his promotion and his group's accomplishments. But he wondered what command would think if they knew how scared and desperate he had been. As far as he was concerned, someone else could have the honor of standing in front of the German war machine.

He took a moment to wash his face and hair and then began inspecting his positions. His tanks were well hidden in depressions about thirty feet below a ridge line. They had spent the better part of the night extending the depression to accommodate the fat, rolling tubs his country labeled as tanks. He had just inspected the last of his six tank crews when he detected a slight tremor under his feet. He gulped down the coffee he was drinking and then started to jog towards his own vehicle. By the time he reached it, the tremor had turned into violent waves. Something big and heavy was coming down the canyon. He left the hatch ajar, hoping to allow the cool air in as long as possible. The first faraway squeaking could just be made out. It was said that the waiting was the worst part; Henry would passionately disagree. The worst part was when somebody was trying his best to kill you. The noise was growing louder by the minute. He had to yell to be heard. "Hey! Hey!"

"What?" his gunner asked.

"At least the air core cleared the skies," Henry said.

"What?" his gunner repeated.

"I said ... Ah forget it."

"What?"

Henry just shook his head. The Germans had to be close now. Henry slammed the lid down and stared down the hill. The canyon made a tight turn, leading the enemy straight toward him. High walls blocked it on three sides, leaving the Germans with two options: retreat or run right over the American tanks. Henry had little faith in the Germans retreating. He was unable to see what was happening around the bend in front of him. The other forces, which would spring the trap, could see for miles.

Finally, the first enemy vehicle came into view: a motorcycle. Henry felt the tension momentarily leave his body and he almost laughed—almost. He watched as the motorcycle came farther into the turn and slowly approached his position. It was his group's responsibility to fire the first shot, but like a good hunter, Henry would wait until more prey had committed themselves and he was assured a good kill before he would spring the trap. Besides, the Americans did not want to reveal the position of their tanks until they had German armor in their sights.

Henry was becoming worried. The motorcycle was already halfway up the cliff and still no other vehicles came into sight. Just when Henry was going to fire, a sniper took out the motorcycle. Henry breathed a sigh of relief and watched the motorcycle disappear into the knee-high grass. Just then, another motorcycle appeared and proceeded toward him at a much faster rate. Evidently, it had fallen too far behind the lead cycle and was in hurry to catch up. *Good thing*, thought Henry. If it had been a few seconds closer, the ambush would have been exposed. As it was, the second cycle sped quickly to its death, falling about twenty yards to the right of its downed brother. Henry could not believe it; the plan had worked. Without air cover and blinded by the unknown loss of their scouts, the Germans were headed straight into jaws of the hungry, salivating American mouth.

The first group of infantry came into view, followed by four German tanks. As these rolled forward, more followed until the entire ground before them was covered in German armor. Henry waited until the tanks were at the site of their fallen scouts and then fired. His tanks fired in groups of three so that two German tanks exploded simultaneously. The Germans were caught off guard and swiveled their guns frantically. The Americans were able to reload and coolly kill their second targets. With all four of the front tanks down, the German infantry swept into motion. Rifleman threw themselves down and began firing up at the ridge line. Bazooka men ran forward, closing the distance. Mortar groups moved behind the fallen tanks and began to set up. The Americans were far more interested in the second group of tanks. And both sides were frantically trying to reload.

For the Germans, the sudden appearance of American tanks and demise of four of their own was crushing. And the Americans were far from the inexperienced green troops they were led to believe they would be. They had turned out to be cold-blooded killers, ruthlessly cutting down their enemy. This too added to the sense of panic that now threatened to overwhelm their lead elements. Had they been able to see what was happening to the rest of the column, they would have indeed been plunged into a gloomy abyss. Their hope lay at the top of the ridge line. If they could successfully break over it, they would be free. With that in mind, the infantry began to rush up the hill.

The six American tanks had taken out two of the four enemy tanks left in their kill zone. The advantage in elevation had paid off—that and their hastily dug earthen walls. They failed to see the danger that the infantry presented. Except for Henry. He threw open the hatch and turned his machine gun on the advancing foot soldiers. His guns sliced through the advancing elements, and then he tried to stop the bazookas. Unfortunately, a small rise in the ground afforded them a shield through which Henry's bullets could not reach them. He realized that if he didn't do something, his tanks would soon die. Henry yelled down, "Keep firing," and then crawled out and ran toward the hump.

He lobbed two grenades and then hit the ground. The explosions threw debris in every direction. Henry jumped up and finished off the threat with his pistol. He began running back to his tank when he felt a burning sensation in his thigh. Henry was having a hard time running when he felt another sting through his shoulder. Stumbling, he felt himself lifted up and above his tank. The whole world seem to be on fire, and then there was nothingness. Luckily, Henry didn't feel the impact as his body slammed back to earth and then rolled down the hill, stopping just a few feet from the burning lead German tank. The battle wasn't a battle after all—just a wholesale slaughter. Henry's tanks never left their original positions, finding plenty of targets right in front of them.

German power in Africa had been broken that day, and nowhere along the five miles of the canyon was it more obvious than at the bend. Fourteen tanks, six halftracks, and one hundred infantry men lay dead and burning. What the British had started, the Americans had finished. Germany was beaten in Africa.

*****

LW smiled as he looked down at Doris. He was standing on his first aircraft carrier, looking over the waiving throng. He could not actually see Doris, but he imagined that he could. After advanced flight school, he had gone back to Texas for weapons training. They had decided to move her back in with her mother while he was away. His orders gave no date of return, and he knew that he would not be home until after the war was won. The ship was slowly maneuvered out from the pier, and within the hour, the shoreline slipped beyond an observer's view. The men began to move into their varying jobs, doing what they had been trained to do, without even having to think about it.

LW soon reported for a preflight meeting. They would begin air operations within the next half hour or so. LW would not fly for several hours; he was in the fourth patrol. After introductions and a brief discussion of the guidelines, the pilots were given housekeeping chores and a list of men under their command. LW was given command over weapons systems. They were dismissed, and LW went below to find his men. After more introductions, LW found out just what weapons systems meant. Far from being fun or exciting, all his men did was check the bomb-release cables and clean the guns. They were also responsible for sweeping and mopping the hanger area. LW took down a list of chores and aircraft and then headed upstairs to his quarters, where he could work in peace.

He could not believe how boring this work was, so when the time came for him to head up to the flight deck, he sighed in relief. The fresh air hit him like a stampeding herd of cows. He sucked it in with gratitude and then caught his first glimpse of his new aircraft, the Hellcat. It was the prettiest thing LW had ever seen. Slick and trim, it looked like what it was: the most advanced killing machine in the world. He slowly walked around it, admiring it, touching it, and finally climbing into it. The crew worked feverishly while LW did his preflight check. After handing his clipboard over, they closed the cockpit and fired up the engine. He was too busy checking gauges and watching for his signals to feel the excitement the roar of the engines should have brought.

When the signal was given, LW revved the engine up to full throttle and then raced down the deck. He felt the aircraft gain lift, and then he was out over the water and climbing. He pointed the nose toward the sky and climbed to his patrol altitude. After a few minutes, he reached a point where he could relax and take a look around. The entire fleet lay below him; ships of varying size and weight stretched out for miles. The horizon melted away in front of him, and the heavens fell off in every direction. He had reached his patrol area and reported in. After that, he had little to do. The Japanese fleets had been mauled, and their carriers were all but wiped out. There was almost no chance that the Americans would be attacked by air this close to the U.S. coastline. The same could be said for an enemy surface vessel. Submarines were an altogether different animal; they could attack anywhere, at any time. He could just make out another fighter about a mile ahead of him and slightly higher. The other Hellcat was heading in roughly the same direction and at the same speed. LW slowly wound his way around his area until he was pointed back over the carrier, and as he looked down on it, he could not believe how tiny it appeared. They had spent many hours practicing landing on a carrier, but nothing had prepared him for sight of a carrier surrounded by open ocean. The very vastness of the water dwarfed the carrier and made it seem insignificant when contrasted with the awe-inspiring panorama spread out before him. When his patrol was over, LW headed back and entered the landing pattern. Only a few planes from each carrier were up at any given time. Still, given that there were four main carriers and six smaller ones, the skies could get awful crowded. He had thought that he would be nervous during his first landing, but again he was so busy that he didn't have time to think about it and made a perfect landing.

Later, at chow, he listened to the older pilots talk about their own experiences in aerial combat with the Japs. The new guys listened and hung on every word. Listening to their stories was entertaining; it was also educational. For this very reason, the navy mixed its veterans with its new recruits. LW finally retreated to his cubby hole and wrote to Doris. He would spend the next few weeks running his men, flying patrols, and scrambling for mock air raids.

When they finally reached Pearl Harbor, he was a seasoned carrier pilot, lacking only combat experience. As they pulled into port, two ships still lay partially submerged, and the entire crew fell silent, knowing that many of their brothers in arms still lay entombed in those vessels. Tears welled up in many an eye and feelings of revenge once again beat in every heart. Other than the stricken vessels, little damage remained from the attack that started this war. They could not help but stare at those silent wonders and remember where they were when they first heard the words *Pearl Harbor*. LW received three days liberty and set out to explore the island. Without question, this was the most beautiful place he had ever seen. Coconuts were a new food to him, and he could not get enough of them. He sipped on one as he walked through downtown Honolulu. The streets were packed with soldiers and sailors from every unit and ship. Everything imaginable was on sale, along with some things that he could not have imagined. Music sounded from every booth, and the constant roar from thousands of military men talking, laughing, and fighting drowned out everything else. He looked skyward and tried to imagine Jap planes screaming down, but the image escaped him. It was simply too tranquil to ever have been a battlefield.

LW walked into a bar and found an empty area near the pool table. He was just having his second beer when a soldier bumped into him, spilling it all over the front of LW's uniform. The soldier turned and told him to watch where he was going. Now LW could not contain his anger and told the soldier where he could go to get his apology. The man answered with a right hook that had no chance of landing. LW ducked under the punch and then landed a combination that left the other man unconscious on the floor. The forty or so other representatives of the army seemed to take offense to this and they began to encircle him. Now, about thirty white shirts weren't going to sit around and watch this happen, and so they too rose and moved in for support.

LW knew he was a superb boxer, but there was no way he was going to win this! All he could see was a sea of green uniforms. His navy comrades were too far back for him to observe. So LW picked up a pool cue, though this was considered dirty fighting, and began slamming it down on heads. Dirty fighting or not, it was highly effective. He quickly cleared the immediate area and began looking for an escape route. The drunken soldiers seemed to be going crazy, falling and fighting each other. LW spotted a path to an exit and began forcing his way to it, slamming his weapon down on any head that tried to bar his path. He had almost reached his destination and freedom when he noticed that a man in a white uniform had just gone down beneath two soldiers. He threw a quick look to the bar and saw what had confused the army guys. His navy pards had come gallantly to his rescue, and though badly outnumbered, they were fighting for all it was worth.

His fellow swabs had come to his rescue, and he could not leave them to fight his battle for him, so he waded back in. The sailors had one distinct advantage: their ships had just arrived and so they were far less into the bottles than the soldiers were. Though fist and feet were the weapons of choice, it wasn't rare to see the occasional bottle or chair go flying by. The owner of the bar made no attempt to break up the melee. He simply made a phone call and then hid himself safely below the bar. Reinforcements began pouring in from outside, and then the fighting spread to the streets.

By the time the first military police arrived, the ruckus had spread over several blocks. The police had been called out to stop a bar fight, not contain a riot. They sat observing the fighting and smacking an occasional combatant on the head. The fact that four out of five heads that they cracked belonged to the navy did not go unnoticed. In moments, their Jeep was overturned and they were fighting for their lives.

Back in the bar, the fighting had all but died out. The owner felt some of his bravery return as the silence grew. He peeked out over the bar and noticed that only two navy men remained on their feet. He surveyed the damage caused by the desperate fight and could barely contain the rage that was building up inside him. He jumped over the bar and grabbed a hold of the two sailors who were weaving drunkenly towards the door. It was his intention that none of them escape punishment. But the minute he laid his hands upon the sailors, he joined the fallen on the floor.

LW helped his wounded friend, who he had recognized earlier in the fight as a fellow fighter pilot. LW propped him up and then headed back to the bar for two bottles of scotch. The other pilot smiled, and the two headed out the door and into freedom.

They could not believe the scene that met their eyes. Smoke billowed up from fires started by the overturned carts of food vendors. Broken carts and shattered stalls littered the streets, along with unconscious sailors and soldiers. From the looks of it, the fighting had been fierce but fairly equal in the number of casualties. Sirens could be heard in all directions and the two hurried across the street and ducked into a saloon, passed through the back door and out into the alley way. It took them three blocks to get free of the riot zone. There, they hailed a cab and left the town behind them. After being dropped off on the beach, they spent the rest of the afternoon killing the bottles of scotch and flirting with whichever girl happened to walk by.

The next day, LW awoke with a terrible headache, and his mouth tasted like a cat had spent the night in it. He rolled over and saw Archie asleep near a pool of vomit. He tried to stand up, but his head swam in different directions, forcing him to sit back down. Finally, he stood and walked down to the water, noticing on the way that he had, at some point, stripped down to his skivvies. The water was refreshing and cool, so he swam around and dove a bit. He was surprised at the depth of the water; though he could see the bottom, he could not swim to it. After a while, Archie swam out and joined him. They decided to get breakfast and walked toward town. They could see a cluster of buildings up ahead and felt their stomachs began to growl. They noticed a Jeep pulling up to them, and they both tensed. It was a military police vehicle. They thought about running and decided that it was too late. The big officer driving looked them up and down.

"You boys spend the night on the beach?"

"As a matter of fact, we did," LW said, holding his head.

"Were you involved in the fighting?"

"What fighting?" Archie asked innocently. "We have been here since yesterday. Now we just want breakfast."

The officers eyed the pilots warily. "How did your face get that way?" the driver asked.

"It isn't his fault. His mother dropped him at birth," LW replied.

"Okay, smart guy, can you tell me what really happened, or would you like to spend some time in the brig?"

"I tried to learn to surf and ended up face down on the rocks. The waves just slammed me straight down to the bottom, and that's the last thing I remember," Archie said with his head cast down in shame.

The officer looked over at LW and said, "I guess you're the hero who saved his life?"

"Yes, sir. I sure am. It must have taken an hour of swimming to fight the current and reach him. I almost got thrown down, too, but I braced myself and was able to avoid it. Without the incredible strength I posses, I never could have done it. That and my willingness to sacrifice for others."

"Okay, that's enough. You two eat breakfast and then report to your ship. Shore leave has been cancelled." The disgusted officer returned to his Jeep and sped off.

"You know, you didn't have to lay it on so thick," LW said, glancing at his friend. Archie tripped and almost fell. He choked out a few choice words and finally gave up and shook his head.

Three weeks later, LW found himself flying a patrol over some island deep in the Pacific. He was watching the water carefully, studying it as he flew over. After more than two weeks at sea, he still had not seen a shark. For some reason, this bothered him, though he did not know why. He decided to mention it to Archie upon their return to the ship. Today Archie was his wingman and flying a short distance behind him. They had to keep radio silence or LW could have asked him then. He felt sure that the lack of sharks was not a good enough reason to give away his position.

A small dot appeared, moving between two of the larger islands. The wake it left behind gave it away; it was a small boat. The American forces had not yet made it this far, so LW signaled to Archie and then began a graceful dive. The rising sun insignia was clearly visible on the small flag. LW opened up with his guns and shot the boat to pieces. He felt his own plane taking hits and climbed to escape the unseen attacker. As he leveled out, it dawned on him what had happened. Archie had followed him down and opened up, spraying bullets that ricocheted from the water up into LW's plane. His engine was starting to cut in and out as he headed back out to sea. Archie was flying back and forth under his plane, taking a look at the damage. He broke radio silence and asked, bewildered, "LW, what did that to you?"

"Fifty calibers," was all LW said. It was all he needed to say. Archie fell silent as he watched the other Hellcat fight to stay in the air. LW could not believe it; he had been shot down, by his own side. The more he thought about it, the madder he got. His plane was getting harder to control, and he began to climb, trying to gain altitude. He was still thirty miles away from the carrier when Archie again broke radio silence.

"You're starting to trail smoke." He could not conceal the worry in his voice.

"Don't you have any good news?" LW replied sharply.

Archie thought for a minute. "The smoke's white," he said hesitantly.

"Good try," LW snapped. His oil pressure was beginning to drop slightly, an indication that he was losing oil somewhere. At least the smoke was white, he thought. His compression wasn't good, and he had to keep the air speed low.

The tower had stayed out of it so far, not wanting to give away its position. The men in the flight control room hung on every word. These were two young pilots, and one was fighting for his life. They both sounded somewhat calm under the circumstances. At fifteen miles out, LW heard a loud grinding noise and then a pop. The plane tried to bank, and it took everything he had to keep it straight. Again Archie's voice sounded over the radio. "A piece of wing just flew off."

"Did you see what piece it was?" LW said through closed teeth.

"It was kinda hard to see at one hundred plus miles per hour," Archie responded.

"Do you mind taking a look?"

"It looks like maybe a one-foot-by-two-foot piece of the skin," he replied. They both were sweating profusely and breathing like they were running a marathon.

"Ten miles out," Archie called. About that time, LW heard another loud pop, and his oil pressure began to dive.

"Black smoke. You're trailing black smoke," Archie cried out.

"Just hold together a while longer. Come on, we're almost home," LW said to his plane.

Back aboard the ship, nervous crewmen listened to the exchange. Though most had never met the pilots, they all felt like their bothers were out there. At seven miles out, sirens began to go off, signaling a wounded bird was inbound. At five miles out, they began descending. LW would have one crack at a landing and would not have enough pressure to try again.

"Okay, LW, we're three miles out. You want to cut down on you air speed?" Archie asked, sounding a little concerned.

"Hell no. If I slow down, I will go down. I need speed or I will lose altitude."

"Oh, sorry about that."

The tower decided to take control and began calling out information and forcing the two pilots to watch their instruments. A mile out and Archie began to break off, moving up and allowing LW all the space he needed. As he approached, LW was watching the signal man and trying to keep his plane level. The black smoke was pouring out of his engine. The signal man was frantically waving him off. LW ignored him and slammed his plane down and gave it full throttle. As he slowly came to a stop, LW hung his head and said a silent prayer of thanks. His engine sputtered and finally died. His plane was sprayed with water and then the canopy was raised. LW half fell and was half dragged out of his plane. He shook everyone off of him and turned to inspect his Hellcat. Holes were shot through both wings, and he was hard pressed to find one square foot of the belly that did not have a hole through it. He watched as they inspected it and then slowly pushed it over the side.

Archie and LW stood on the deck and observed as their ship pulled into a small island.

"I wonder if this is the same island where you shot me down," LW said.

"Well, if you were half the pilot I was, then you wouldn't have been shot down," Archie said sarcastically.

"Technically, I wasn't shot down; I made it back to the ship."

"Only because I showed mercy." They both laughed and headed down below. They were do a little shore leave time, and they could not wait to find out what the island had to offer. Both were stunned to find out that the island was uninhabited.

"What kinda shore leave is this? What are we supposed to do on a island with no people? Why would we even stop here? Is this some kinda punishment?" Archie was flabbergasted.

"Maybe it is punishment. What do you expect them to do with someone who shoots down his friends? Maybe give them a parade?" LW said with a sneer.

"Now we've been through that. Technically I didn't shoot you down," Archie said defensively. Just then, about five sailors ran past them and headed down the ramp.

"Where do you think they're going?" LW asked no one in particular. One of the men yelled over his shoulder that the captain was allowing them to go swimming. LW thought about that a moment and then ran to his room to change. He met Archie and five other pilots down at the ramp, and they all jumped in. The water felt cool, and they began diving and swimming toward the beach.

One of the other pilots looked over at LW and asked, "Why didn't you put down in the water instead of risking a crash?"

"I was worried about sharks," he replied. All the pilots nodded in agreement and then slowly looked around.

"I didn't think about that," Archie said.

"Me either," one of the other pilots replied.

A sailor was swimming by and noticed the strange expressions written on their faces. "What's up? Looks like you guys saw a ghost."

"We just thought about all the sharks and how we're lined up like a feast," LW said.

The sailor pointed up to the ship and laughed. "What do you think those guys with rifles are for?"

"What are you saying?" Archie inquired.

"Those guys are on shark duty."

The pilots were quickly lost in thought. LW started swimming slowly toward the beach.

"Hey, LW, don't you think swimming in shark-infested water is insane?" Archie yelled.

"Not as insane as flying an aircraft off a tiny boat at two hundred miles per hour. Or flying hundreds of miles just to get shot at," LW replied.

Everyone smiled and started swimming after him. LW stood on the beach in his sopping wet tennis shoes and stared at the concrete bunker. Its size wasn't all that impressive, but this was as close to the enemy as he had ever been. He watched as barely visible smoke still floated lazily from the black window. As he approached the shattered bunker, he took note of the scattered bullet and shrapnel holes. They stared back at him like silent, dead eyes. He felt a chill as he rounded the corner and stared into the dark maw that was its doorway. As he entered, he could still faintly smell gun powder and charred flesh. The evidence of the ferocity of the battle that raged on this tiny island was strewn inside the bunker. Bloody bandages and empty ammunition cans lay in piles. Empty casings lay scattered over the floor. The walls and ceilings were scorched black. Almost every item in the room was charred. He could not force himself to move farther into the room. Through the windows, he could see the fleet at anchor, and he could hear the approach of his friends. The laughter and cat calls were a far cry from the yelling and screaming that had so recently echoed from the concrete walls. As he turned to go, something in the corner caught his eye. He walked over to it and saw something red sticking out from under an ammo box. He could make out a small bundle of paper items. A picture glued to a red piece of cardboard was on the bottom. Leary of a booby trap, he gently pulled the packet out. Most of it appeared to be letters, written in Japanese.

He left the bunker and headed down the beach. The other pilots had just raided a small boat that had ferried in from one of the tenders. They secured a football and some beer. LW took one as he headed down the beach, looking for a somewhat secluded spot to further investigate his find. Locating a large boulder jutting out over the water, he climbed up and removed the ribbon holding the bundle together. As he first concluded, the bulk of his find was indeed letters. There was also some money—Japanese money of course. But it was the picture that held his attention. It was of a small woman wearing traditional robes and smiling as she held an umbrella. She was pretty but not stunningly so. He wondered briefly what she was like. Was she a sister, girlfriend, or wife? Probably not a wife; she was too young. Then he remembered how young Doris was. He considered the probable fate of the packet's owner and quickly felt remorse. There was little room in his present attire to hide the bundle from prying eyes. Tucking away the package in his shorts, he headed back to his friends and a cookout on the beach. LW could not put his whole heart into the games they were playing. The haunting memory of a smiling woman in robes stayed with him.

*****

Henry awoke to find himself lying in a tent. His head hurt, and he had a bad case of cotton mouth. He had no idea where he was or how he got there. The last thing he could remember was running toward his tank. His memory of those events was fuzzy. He noticed an object hanging from his sheet, and on closer inspection, he identified it as a medal—a purple heart to be exact. "Holy crap, was I shot?" He began a frantic search for any new holes. He found two suspicious areas but was unable to confirm the extent of the damage due to the bandages. When he tried to stand up, Henry learned two things almost simultaneously. The first was that his head was bandaged as well and did not seem to be working properly. The second was that his arms had tubes stuck in them, and he would have to remove them to have any chance of standing. He heard yelling, which sounded muffled, and raised his head, which caused lights to explode in a crazy display before his eyes. He became nauseated and tried to lay back down. He felt small hands upon his shoulders and looked into the face of a very small and angry woman, dressed in white. *An angel*, he thought, *an angry angel*. She was yelling at him in a weird, muffled voice. He was trying to explain that he could not understand her, when she did something very un-angel like. She reached between his legs and pulled out a pan of some kind. Henry was taken aback; who had ever heard of an angel doing that? Before he could organize his thoughts, the angry angel yelled at him again and then stuck him. He howled in protest and tried to sit up again. This angel was not only angry; she was also crazy. She stuck him again. He then noticed the arrival of someone else and tried to warn him about the insane angel and her stinger. Before he could, Henry's eyes slowly closed.

When he awoke, he was in the same confused state as before. He still had no idea where he was or how he got there. He did remember that mean angel, and so he lay quietly, hoping not to incur her wrath again. He noticed that everyone here was talking in a muffled language. He concentrated on the person lying next to him. It appeared to be a soldier playing cards. An angel was standing at the foot of the soldier's bed, and they were having a conversation. Henry was so engrossed with the scene next to him that he failed to notice the arrival of his angel. The first indication of her presence was when she tried to stick something into his mouth. He thought about biting her but then recalled her last tantrum and decided to try to appease her instead. After a few minutes, she removed the stick from his mouth and then concentrated on it. She seemed satisfied and smiled at him. It was the most beautiful smile he had ever seen. He made up his mind that he would endure everything she wanted if she would reward him with a smile.

Later, she came back with some food, and he ate with a vengeance. He had not realized how hungry he really was. After he finished, he managed to ask her if she was an angel. She flashed him the biggest grin to date and answered in that muffled language that everyone seemed to speak around here. The angel seemed to be trying to get his attention, and when he looked at her, she pointed to her hat. He noticed the red cross on it for the first time. He slowly took in this new information and everything it implied. She was a nurse, which meant that this was a field hospital, which in turn meant that he had indeed been shot. He was still trying to come to terms with this when she reached up under him again. This time, instead of feeling indignation, he turned the same shade of red as her cross. She wrote something on a piece of paper and held it up for his inspection. He tried to focus on it and realized he only had one eye. Panic coursed through his body as his hands reached for his nonresponding eye. She caught his hands and gently shook her head no, and again pointed toward the paper. He tried again, and this time the words finally came into focus.

"You have been wounded. I am a nurse. You cannot use your eye yet, and you have lost your hearing." Henry reached for her pen and quickly began to write. She covered his hand, took the pen back, and wrote something else. She again held the page before him. "You have lost your hearing, not your voice."

"Oh, sorry about that," he said. "How badly am I injured?"

She wrote his answer down and the handed it back. "You were shot twice. Once through the leg and once through the shoulder. A mortar or tank round exploded close to you and propelled you through the air. That's how your head was injured and why you lost your hearing."

"Will I be able to hear again?"

"Yes," she wrote.

"Will I be able use my eye again?"

She scribbled quickly and then stood up. "I don't know. Now I have other patients to see. Do you need anything?"

"I would like to write a letter, and I would like some ice cream if you have it." She smiled again and nodded. Henry smiled back and then watched as she walked away.

He must have dozed off, because when he opened his eyes, she was standing before him with paper and a pen. They beamed at each other and then she held up a bowl of strawberry ice cream. Henry could not believe it. Here he was, in the middle of, well he wasn't sure about where, but he was being hand-fed strawberry ice cream by a gorgeous nurse. He had no idea where LW was, but he knew the very idea of his situation would turn him green with envy. He looked into her eyes as she fed him; it was her turn to blush. Henry did not try to speak until all the ice cream had been consumed.

"Thank you," he managed.

She grinned and then began writing. It seemed like she was writing forever. Finally, she finished with her essay and handed it over to him. "My name is Tabitha; people call me Tabby. I am from Wyoming. I all ready know your name, Henry. We are in Morocco, North Africa. You have been wounded but not terribly so. I have twenty patients under my care. You were brought in yesterday evening. It is now nighttime, so you have been here for one day. I don't really know what is going on in the war, but I did hear that you guys won a big battle. Not many wounded men have arrived, so the doctors say it must have been pretty one-sided."

"How long have you been in the army?" Henry asked.

She started laughing. "I am not in the army," she wrote.

"How long have you been in Africa?"

"About six weeks. What do you do?" she wrote.

"Do? What do you mean?" Henry asked.

"In the army, what is it that you do?"

"Oh, I am in tanks."

"In them? Do you mean that you drive them?"

"No, I'm actually a tank commander."

"Really? How many tanks do you command?"

"Three, or at least I did have three."

"What did the general mean by 'his anvil'?"

"I don't know. What general?"

"This morning a general came by and pinned on those medals. He called you his anvil."

Henry's head hurt too much to think about it. She noticed his pain and went to get something. When she returned, he noticed that she was carrying a syringe. He tried to wave her off but she refused to concede. After she administered the painkiller, she wrote that she would visit him in the morning. By the time she walked out of his view, he was sound asleep.

Chapter Nine

Doris had been home for six months, and she was about to pull her hair out. Not that her parents had changed their behavior; she was the one who had changed. After having her own home, she was having a hard time adjusting to living under her parents' roof again. She was spending more and more time with her in-laws. Her mother-in-law treated her like a daughter. They cooked and cleaned together, and of course shopped together. News from the war poured in on almost an hourly basis. She tried hard not to think about her loved ones as the different battle reports were read. This morning, her and Annie were cooking pies when they saw the mailman walking up the sidewalk. LW's mother called out through the open window.

"You bringing anything good today, Hal?"

"Oh, just some bills and a Sears catalogue."

"Well at least we can dream about some new curtains."

"They have some nice ones in here. By the way, do you want me to put all these letters from LW in there, too?" he added with a smile. There was silence from the window as the two women took this startling revelation in. "Hello, are you there?" Hal called out questioningly. The front door exploded open and LW's mother ran out and slapped Hal on the arm.

"How could you, Hal?"

"Now, Annie, I was just teasing a bit."

There were nine letters all together. Four for each of the women, and one for his father. Doris took her letters and retreated to the back porch. She tore the first one open and tears began to roll down her cheeks. His mother was going through the same process on her bed. When LW Sr. arrived home, he found his wife in tears. He asked what had happened, and she just waved him off. He walked into the kitchen for a glass of milk and noticed Doris sitting outside. "What in the hell is going on here?" He stuck his head out the back door.

"How are you doing today?" Doris looked up and smiled. The tears were evident on her cheeks as well.

"Somebody better tell me what's going on," he bellowed. His concern was growing. He retraced his footsteps back into the bedroom. "Annie, talk to me. Did something happen to LW?" She shook her head no and tossed his letter to him. He tore it opened and walked back to the kitchen table. His son had written of life in the navy—the hair-raising landings in the pouring rain, the violent storms and wind shears. He told his father about the dog fighting and the anti-aircraft fire. The story of the fistfight in Hawaii brought a smile to his face. He grew more serious as he read about Archie shooting up LW's plane and the fight to get back to the carrier. If LW had written about these things to his mother and wife, then they were in for a rough time. His son's closing sentence relieved his concern.

"I didn't write to Doris or mom about any of this. I thought it might upset them." LW Sr. exhaled and thanked God that he had raised a thoughtful boy. He went into the bedroom and saw that his wife still had two letters left to read. He quietly shut the door and walked back into the kitchen. Doris, he observed, still had three unopened letters. He went into the living room and turned on the radio. The news drowned out the two crying females in the background. LW Sr. sipped his milk as the commentator droned on, "Allied forces continued to pound the coast of Sicily as ground forces quickly overwhelmed the Axis's beach defense."

*****

Henry had enjoyed his time with Tabby. He had spent three weeks recovering from his wounds and another six weeks rehabilitating himself. His sight and hearing had gradually returned to normal, and his limp was barely noticeable. He was to rejoin his unit in Sicily the following week. He had spent most of his time in the company of his nurse, and they had quickly fallen for each other. Henry could not wait for the war to end. He half hoped that the Germans would come to their senses and stop this war. But with a madman at the helm, he knew that it was unlikely. The fighting could drag on for years. He spent the next few days running and swimming and seeing Tabby every chance he got. When the day came for him to ship out, he said good-bye with genuine regret. He boarded the truck and waved until she was out of sight. That night, he crossed the Mediterranean and rejoined the war.

*****

Billy was worn out. This was his fifth island landing. He had been fighting since the war began. Very few of his original company were left. As a matter of fact, he had heard only 5 percent had made it this far. He didn't want to think about all that had been lost. He just wanted to go home, and every island brought him closer to that elusive goal. He had received a letter from LW; it had arrived just days before they hit the beach. As usual, LW highlighted all the advantages he was enjoying. To hear him tell it, life on a carrier was like being at a country club: a hot bath and a hot meal every day, plenty of sightseeing, and a lot of fishing. Billy laughed out loud; his cousin was so full of himself. Still, he had to believe the part about the hot baths and hot food. Billy had not had a bath in three days and he could not remember his last hot meal. He knew that today he would get that shower and the meal. The battle was over, and the cleaning up process was almost complete. So this evening, the army would have a cookout and set up showers. Sometimes the navy boys joined them, but most of the time it was only those who took part in the actual fighting.

The men lined up for the showers, and Billy pushed his way to the front of the line. He was a veteran among veterans, and they made room for him. The water was almost boiling hot, and Billy loved it. Three days of grime, three days of gun smoke, and three days of blood washed down under the pallets. Each man got a five-minute shower, and it was five minutes of heaven on earth. That done, Billy put on a clean pair of pants and a clean shirt. When he finished shaving, he felt like a new man. He headed over to the chow line and learned they were serving chili dogs, pork and beans, and potato salad. There was another surprise: along with the beer, they had lemonade. Even though they knew that it had come from a can, it was still the best lemonade any of them could remember. Billy fell asleep on the beach, his stomach full and his body clean. One more fight and one less. It had to end soon … it had to.

*****

LW was getting frustrated. He had been flying forever and had not even seen one Japanese machine—not one plane, not one ship, not even a raft. The lack of targets was becoming the norm. He guessed that Japan must be out of aircraft. Today he was Archie's wingman, and the temptation for revenge crept into his thoughts as it did each and every time he flew wingman for Archie.

As a new day dawned, the chances of encountering enemy aircraft increased, for every day they inched closer to the imperial Japanese homeland. They had come to the end of their patrol and were about to turn around when Archie flashed his wings and pointed down. LW looked toward the water's surface and noticed a twin-engine craft passing on an intersecting course below them. Archie began a series of dives that took them ever closer to their possible prey. As they closed in, there could be no mistake: the rising sun insignia was staring at them from each wing. Archie moved into attack position and began firing in rapid succession. LW followed, and the plane slowly nosed over. Both engines were ablaze, and debris flew off the stricken plane. Both Hellcats watched as it made it's final dive into the sea.

Just as the splash hid the craft from view, LW was covered in glass. Rounds bounced of his plane, and tracer rounds made their way from his plane over to Archie's. LW dove and pulled to the right just in time to see two Zeros go roaring by. As he recovered, he searched the surrounding sky, looking for more Zeros. He spotted three more up high and to his port. The other two were climbing, probably maneuvering for a second go at them. It was then that he noticed Archie's plane. It was trailing black smoke and was losing altitude. Even as he watched, it inverted and nosedived. LW had been barking warnings into his radio. Now he screamed, "Archie, pull up! Archie!" He watched in horror as his friend dove straight down and crashed into the sea. He had little time to mourn; the other Zeros were closing fast. The tower assured him that help was on its way, but given the distance, they probably would not make it in time. LW dove left and then circled back and up, climbing parallel to his previous course. The Zeros had broken into two groups, and each tried to match LW's moves. The Hellcat was much faster and more agile, but numbers were on their side. LW finally got some altitude and saw the group of three maneuvering to get behind him. He turned and dove, climbed, and then banked hard and dove again. This time, when he climbed, they were all over him. Because of his breakneck maneuvering, they were also out of position and their shots flew wild. LW closed in behind them and gave one a full burst. He was rewarded by a plume of black smoke and then a ball of fire. He quickly banked hard again and climbed. The group of two had managed to maneuver behind him, and when he banked, they came in fast. All three aircraft opened up in a head-on duel. As they passed each other, LW pulled up, but not before he saw pieces fly off of one of the Zeros. At the same time, he felt his own plane take hits. He looked around to see if he was clear to make a run for it; then he spotted two Zeros above him.

He watched as one began to dive. So LW dove and forced the other plane to bank. This was buying him time, but the outcome was never really in doubt. LW could not last much longer. He radioed in his position and the number of remaining enemy aircrafts. He was approaching the point of no return. That meant that in moments, he would not have enough fuel to make it back to the carrier. He was also out of airspace. They had succeeded in forcing him to the ocean's surface. He took the only option left open to him: he ran. Though his Hellcat was much faster, the Zero would match his speed by diving. He made it all of one minute. Then the Zeros came in and tore into his plane. LW felt the impact and was then sprayed with oil. He cut his airspeed and lowered his flaps. He worked his levers and tried to nurse his engines. It was no use; his bird was dead. Smoke and flames were engulfing his plane. LW sent out a mayday call and headed for water.

The inbound group of American fighters were still five minutes away. Their frustration at not being able to help their comrade was heightened when they received his distress call.

The Zeros were running out of fuel, and they knew that these two American planes were not alone out here. They broke off and headed home.

LW braced himself for the impact. "Damn, this is going to hurt," he muttered just before his plane hit the water and skipped across the surface. He had been able to drop his airspeed to fifty-eight miles per hour. By skipping across the water, he lost speed and eased the impact. When his plane came to rest, it immediately began filling up with water. He had only seconds to unhook from his harness and release the canopy. He freed himself and then pushed up, and nothing happened. He tried again and still nothing happened. Turning in his seat, he got his legs up and kicked with everything he had. The canopy moved about four inches. Water was quickly filling the cockpit and the Hellcat was about to take its final dive. Panicking, he began to kick harder, and at last it opened. LW scrambled out as the water poured in. Seconds later, his Hellcat disappeared in a circle of bubbles and he was left alone in the vast emptiness of the open ocean.

He gripped his flotation device and waited. A few moments later, he heard the droning of approaching aircraft. He felt both elated and angry—angry because the Zeros were gone and elated because he was not alone. The Hellcats flew high, searching for the enemy, finding none. Half the group broke for the water, trying to locate their lost pilots. LW fished out his flare and waved his arms. Finally, they saw him and began flying over. Soon just one aircraft remained circling overhead. He could see the rest of the Hellcats searching back along the trail of the fight. He realized they were looking for Archie. He knew with a sinking heart that Archie had gone down with his plane. He could only hope that his friend was dead before the impact. The Hellcats continue to fly around him, unable to rescue him. They were becoming dangerously low on fuel but were reluctant to leave a downed brother. Flight control understood and even sympathized with them. But they were not going to lose any more planes today and ordered them to return. With a final wave of his wings, the last plane headed back to the fleet.

LW watched until he could no longer see the craft. Loneliness set in. Though he knew why they left, it still didn't make it any easier. LW had been reduced to flotsam as he floated helplessly, completely at the mercy of the ocean. After an hour, he started to grow tired. His eyes were burning, and he had minor cuts that were bothersome but not fatal. Thankfully, most of the bleeding had stopped. He was observing a nasty cut on his hand when a small drop of blood rolled down his finger and fell into the water. He watched it dissipate and saw a shadow pass below him. Its meaning dawned on him, and the horror of it sank in. He was a floating, bleeding piece of meat. He kicked out aggressively and turned in circles, looking for what he prayed wouldn't be there. There was nothing to see, just empty ocean. LW grew thirsty, and the salt stung his wounds and his eyes. The sun beat down on him, and the reflecting light was slowly blinding his already tender eyes.

He had been hearing a noise for a while when it occurred to him what it was. He frantically searched the heavens for the aircraft he knew was there. His eyes refused to focus. Cursing, he reached for his flare gun and fired it in the air. A minute later, an aircraft came swooping down on him. In the past, LW had made fun of the ugly "flying boats" as they were called. But today it was the most beautiful plane he had ever seen. It circled a few times and then landed about a hundred yards away. LW started swimming towards it when he saw the door open and a raft appear. He tried not to choke down salt water as he desperately watched the crewman climb aboard. He had only been in the water for a few hours, but it felt like days.

All of the sudden, he felt a tug on his boot. "Son of a bitch!" He started kicking with all his might. His foot came loose and LW frantically reached for his pistol. The rescue boat was fast approaching, when the downed pilot pulled a side arm and began shooting into the water. The sailor almost stopped the boat, and then he put two and two together. He could hear the pilot's insane screaming: "You come back and I'll kill you!" LW was about to stick his head under water for a better shot when he heard the boat pull up. The rescuer started to move forward to assist him into the boat when LW came lunging over the side. He raised his pistol and fired two more rounds at the water.

"Back up. I think I see him under the boat." The sailor stared at LW. He could not believe that this man who had just been rescued cared more about killing the shark then getting out of there.

"Didn't you hear me? He's coming back." The sailor gave it gas and turned to head back to the plane.

"That's it, just a little farther." LW was bent over the front of the boat, taking careful aim. "Just a little closer, closer. I got you, you bastard." *Click.* The gun was empty. Now overwhelmed with anger, LW began feeding his extra clip into the pistol. The sailor could not believe his eyes. His rescued pilot was bent over the front of the boat in order to get a better shot at a shark. He watched as LW tried to fire his gun and then glanced where LW was trying to shoot. A twelve-foot great white swam by, eyeing the boat.

"Turn around. I'll get him on the next pass."

"What?" said a confused would-be rescuer.

"You have to turn around if we are going to get another shot at him," LW replied calmly.

"After all that, you want to turn around? We aren't turning around. We're getting the hell out of here," replied the incredulous sailor.

"Look, I know I blew my shot back there. I should have checked the gun. But that's no reason to act like this."

The sailor shook his head as they pulled up to the plane. LW acknowledged that he wasn't going to get his revenge by shouting a few choice words at the unseen shark.

Once on the plane, LW sat shaking in the corner. He could not believe that the ordeal was over. The medics went to work on him, cleaning him up and doing a quick exam. When the got to his feet, they saw that one boot was partially gone. The bone in his foot appeared to be protruding from the skin. Upon closer examination, they found the bone was actually a tooth—a shark tooth. They stared in amazement and then removed the remaining portions of the boot.

LW was starting to feel the effects of the morphine they had just given him. His mind was reeling from the trauma of the crash and the shark attack. "Hell of a day. Hell of a day," he mumbled. "I was attacked by Japs, then crashed into the ocean, and was bit by a shark. Hell of a day. Wait until I tell Archie about this." Something came to the back of his mind, something he knew but could not focus on it. Oh well; it probably didn't matter. He heard someone say something about loss of blood, but it was too far away to make out clearly.

LW was in and out of consciousness throughout the trip back to the ship. They kept him conscious while the doctor removed the tooth and finished cleaning all of the cuts he had received. By the time the doctor finished sewing, LW had over one hundred sutures. After he was wrapped up, he was moved to a bed and given enough painkillers to sleep. He dreamed of burning planes and giant sharks. When he awoke the next morning, it was to the sobering reality that he had lost another friend. He was allowed to hobble around the ship and given time to come to terms with what had happened. His reaction to the shark was shrugged off as shock. LW did not comment, but his heart still beat with the thoughts of revenge. The loss of Archie made LW feel worn out. Though they had only flown together for a short period of time, their bond had been strengthened by the stress of war. He kept the shark tooth on his dresser and spent hours studying it. His dreams were a mess of images that he could barely remember in the mornings. But the one that stuck with him was of an enormous shark, slowly circling him, watching with those dead eyes.

It was three weeks before he was cleared for flying. The tower was concerned about his ability to get over his crash. So today was a test flight in every sense of the word. But if they were looking for signs of stress, they were very disappointed. He made a perfect takeoff and an uneventful flight, followed by his usual picture-perfect landing. The flight did little to bring him peace. If anything, it focused his anger, and his thoughts became more hostile. His chance for revenge presented itself the following morning. He and six other Hellcats were sent to bomb and strafe a Japanese island. The skies had been cleared of enemy aircraft, and the island was an unprotected, target-rich environment. They spotted a runway and fuel depot, and in a matter of minutes, the entire facility was a smoking caldron of burning fuel. Firing at anything even remotely questionable, the planes were like the hand of fate striking without warning. Villages were not spared their wrath, and before darkness fell, every building and hut had been thoroughly sliced up.

That night, LW sat watching as the fleet began its bombardment. As the big guns shredded the once beautiful island, he felt his anger fade. He no longer wanted revenge; his anger had turned to disgust. LW just wanted to go home. Too much blood, too much sweat, and far too much death had taken their toll. Gone was the innocence of youth. LW took one long, wary look and then turned and, without a backward glance, headed for his bunk.

*****

Henry had rejoined his division in Italy. They had fought up the boot and into the heart of Europe itself. Now they were sitting on the side of a road, eating dinner from a can. It was raining hard, and Henry had positioned a tarp over the top of the hatch. The stink of oil and fuel inside the tank made his stomach turn. Besides, there wasn't much of a chance that German troops would show up. They were all cut off in cities, fighting for their lives. Most of his men were upset that they had been stopped from advancing to Berlin. The politicians had decided to let the Russians take the German capital. His troops felt it was a disgrace, Henry disagreed. In fact, earlier he had told them exactly how he felt. He said the war was all but over; just the cities remained. The Germans were well dug in and fighting for their families and homes. They would fight to the death, as the Americans would do if the situation was reversed. The cities would be slaughter zones, with brutal house by house fighting. The Germans were whipped. The war was all but over, and Henry was happy about it. If the Russians wanted to expend all those lives so they could have the honor of taking Berlin, than let them have at it. He would be satisfied staying right there on the side of the road and finishing out the war in relative peace and safety.

After that, his men had become silent, thinking through his words. Some of them went into the small town they were helping guard and bought some beer. Henry lay on top of the tank, watching rain run down his tarp, drinking some of the recently purchased beer, and listening to the radio. His music was suddenly interrupted by an urgent bulletin. Hitler was dead, and the new German leader had surrendered. Henry felt tears running down his cheeks as he screamed out in relief. Up and down the road, guns were fired and men were dancing.

*****

LW was playing ping pong when the captain called for their attention. "Gentlemen, we have just received word from Europe. Hitler is dead, and the war in Europe is over. I know this is exciting news, but let's remember our fight is only halfway done." LW found himself smiling and praying that Henry was alive and hearing this news in good health.

The fleet had not been involved with the fighting on Iwo Jima. They had been moving slowly toward Tokyo, closing down the last of the shipping lanes. Patrols had become stressful again as wave after wave of suicide planes flew in. The Hellcats frantically searched in ever-widening circles. Sometimes they caught the kamikazes and quickly dispatched them, but more often than not, the planes got through. It was damn hard to defeat a fighter that refused to stay and fight. The whole world knew that, like Germany, Japan was beat. But like their allies, the Japanese refused to see the inevitable. They were determined to fight on, against the whole world, until they had none to send against their enemies.

*****

Billy lay hunkered down in his recently dug hole. Rumor had it that the Japanese were going to airlift reinforcements onto the island. How they could accomplish this with so many U.S. navy planes around, he had no idea. But that is what they were told was going to happen. So Billy and company were digging in. He did not understand what was taking the Japs so long to surrender. The Italians had given up the fight long ago, and even the Germans had finally seen the light. The Japanese, on the other hand, seemed bound and determined to hammer it out to the very end. He was under no illusions on what the fight for their homeland would be like. Every island that they had hit had been harder to take than the one before it. His luck had held out thus far, but he was pretty sure it would not hold through an invasion of the main island. Lots of Americans would die, and in the end, far more Japanese would perish. This would be an epic battle, perhaps the largest ever fought. Only a miracle would save the world from such a colossal tragedy.

Just after dark, the invasion began. Billy knew this because every naval ship for miles around let loose with everything it had. Explosions began rocking the island. All the entrenched soldiers could do was hunker down.

"I didn't think that the Japanese had any surface ships left," said one of the soldiers sharing Billy's hole.

"Why are you asking?" Billy thought the question irrelevant under the circumstances.

"For a destroyed fleet, they are sure shelling the hell out of this island."

"And they sure don't have much of a pattern," piped in another soldier. Billy had to agree with them. The shells—and that's definitely what they were—were sporadic and ineffective. They seemed to be landing here and there with no specific purpose. Tracers cut through the sky and then stopped or turned in different directions. Though Billy had to admit this was his first time being shelled from sea, it still seemed wrong. There should be some sort of pattern. It was a moonless night, the tracers and explosions being the only source of light. As the shelling slacked off, they began to hear screaming and shouting. It sounded close, but the clear ocean air could carry sound pretty far.

"I'll bet a ship went down," one soldier concluded.

"Sounds like a party to me," another soldier stated.

"Wounded men floating in dark, salty water sometimes lose their minds," the first soldier replied.

"They haven't been in the water that long," the second soldier shot back.

"Be quiet. I hear something," Billy said sternly. They all listened carefully to the strange happenings going on below them. Finally, they could all hear it plainly: a band was playing music.

"Now what could that be about?" Billy said out loud. "What the hell is going on down there?"

"I have no idea," the younger soldier replied.

"He wasn't asking you!" the other soldier said.

"Would you two shut up?" Billy yelled. A shroud of silence descended on their little group.

Three more tense hours passed before a messenger arrived. Billy didn't tell him how close he had come to being shot.

"You boys heard the news?" he asked.

"The mailman seems to be running late," the young soldier said.

The messenger eyed him for a moment and then turned to Billy. "We just dropped two atomic bombs on Japan."

"What's an atomic bomb?" the young soldier asked.

"It's a big bomb," the messenger replied.

"So what?" the young soldier asked, confused.

"It blew the hell out of them, that's what."

"So what? What does it mean?"

"Are you stupid or something?" the messenger asked the young soldier.

Billy had had enough. He grabbed the messenger by the throat. "He means, what does it mean to us? Tell us now or we will shoot you and say the Japs did it."

"Okay, you don't have to get rough." Billy moved his rifle up menacingly. "The Japs have had enough. They're calling it quits," the messenger replied. Then he remembered that he had a lot more soldiers to break the news to and perked up.

"You're not just pulling my leg, are you?"

"No, it's over," he replied as he got to his feet and headed out of the hole.

"What was up with the navy boys last night?" Billy inquired

"They found out about it last night, and to celebrate, they opened up with everything they had. Even managed to get the band playing," the messenger yelled over his shoulder as he dashed towards another hole.

The soldiers sat on the rim of their hole and stared at each other. None of them could believe that the fighting was over. No more tromping through bug-infested swamps or climbing hills with machine guns firing at them. Billy had to admit he felt a little let down. Now maybe if they had known the night before and been able to join in the festivities, maybe he would feel better. It didn't seem right that it was just over. He had to stop and think about it—four years of his life and it was just like that it was over.

The soldiers in the hills seemed to be forgotten as the brass moved from war operations to occupation. For three days, they sat in and around their holes, until the evening of the third day. Then another messenger appeared with orders for Billy to report to the beach. So he said a quick good-bye and jumped into the back of a waiting Jeep. He was rushed down the hill. He joined others in a shower line and was given new clothes and fed. He and the other men were then loaded on a waiting ship, and no sooner had the last of them stepped on board then the vessel began to head out to sea. The entire trip from his hole in the hillside to the deck of this ship lasted about an hour. Billy finally asked an officer where they were going. The officer smiled and said, "We're taking you home. All the vets with four or more years are catching the first ride home." Billy could not believe it; just like that it was over. He left home four years ago, planning to serve his one year and be done with it. Billy had not complained about the added three years; his country needed him, period. Now his country was safe, and he was at last a free man. He could not wait to see Katy, Henry, and LW again.

*****

LW was thinking over his work plan for his men when the news was announced. He heard the cheers and paused for a moment and then went back to work. Later that day, he sat alone, staring out across the ship's wake. He couldn't help thinking about the war's end and what it meant. He was elated at the idea of going home, seeing his family, holding Doris, and going hunting with the guys. But a sense of sadness kept pushing its way in. Was it worth the cost, the terrible, terrible cost? The list of the names he knew personally kept running through his mind: Archie, Harold ... not to mention the millions and millions that he didn't know. And for what? The three countries that started this war had come to ruin, gaining nothing for all the horror they brought into this world. LW felt his stomach turn. He was at a loss for words.

He felt rather than heard someone come up beside him. The head of air operations had listened to the ship celebrating and had come down here to be alone with his thoughts. He noticed the pilot sitting cross-legged and wondered why he was not inside with the rest of the crew.

"Don't feel like celebrating?" he asked the young pilot.

LW looked up. "Just remembering old friends."

This was what the man had suspected. "A lot of old friends are gone. And we should always remember, but we must not forget that they fell serving their country and giving their all for this victory."

LW thought about that for a moment. "Yes, sir, but I can't help thinking what a waste this war was."

"War usually is a waste, but good nations must stand against evil, and when they do, they need good men to fight for them." LW nodded his head and looked back out to sea. After a while, the officer left LW to his memories. Alone, LW finally let it out, crying like a baby.

The next morning, he took off and joined up with three other Hellcats. Their assignment was to fly over the coast of mainland Japan. When he saw the coastline, his nerves started to settle. He had a mission, and that's all that mattered. As they flew down the coast, they flew over small villages and big towns. He could not see the faces of the people, but he could see them run out and stare up at him. As he flew over a factory, he was amazed to see row after row of brand-new fighter planes. He had a mental picture of a Japan that resembled a burned-out Germany. The truth was that it looked like a normal country should look. The temptation of all those aircraft lined up was almost unbearable. The Hellcats looped around and headed back over the town. It looked from the ground as if they were lining up for a shot, or at least that was what LW hoped. Their orders were not to engage unless they were shot at first. He could see people running below, but to his disappointment, they appeared to be running for shelter. He banked hard and dove straight at the parked planes. He gave them every second he could to fire at him. There had to be at least one hothead among them. Finally, he pulled up at the last second, skimmed over the hangar's roof, and then turned and flew out towards the port.

The four planes flew at treetop level, and when they reached the port, they were surprised to see a fleet of ships tied up at the docks. Frigates, destroyers, and tender ships lay silent at their moorings. In growing frustration, the American fighters circled the helpless targets.

However, low on fuel and not receiving any resistance, they reluctantly headed back out to sea. LW was happy to see two destroyers headed into port and decided to buzz them, only to find out they were American warships, coming to claim the naval yard. The American fighter groups, trained and equipped with deadly intention, hardened by war, suddenly found themselves flying over a sea of tranquility. Like the previous years, the sea was full of warships and the skies were full of planes; unlike previous years, they were all American. The only excitement was when a Russian destroyer entered Japanese waters. They flew over it and around it, and did everything they could to provoke a fight. All it earned them was a reprimand. LW came to the decision that things had gone from dull to outright boring. The navy had come to the same conclusion. There simply wasn't a threat to deal with in any ocean anywhere in the world. The seas had been swept clean of enemy ships. Now their biggest worry was the boredom of millions of American service men.

*****

Henry was dumbstruck. After Germany surrendered, he thought the war was over for him and his men. But the officer before him said the army had other ideas. Japan was proving to be as stubborn as Germany. The army needed experienced, battle-ready troops. Henry's tanks were well-rested and in good shape. As soon as their equipment could be made ready, they were to ship out for the Pacific. Henry fought the urge to choke the man who had brought the orders. But there would simply be another officer, and another, and another. He simply could not kill all of them. So he took his orders, saluted, and went to spread the good news. He blamed his new assignment on his obviously incompetent cousins. Henry had won his war; they should have won theirs.

Henry found himself on board a ship heading to someplace in the Pacific. They only had a vague idea about where they were going. But they had an excellent notion as to where they would end up: Japan. Every day they were briefed on the conditions of the islands and Japanese tactics and arms. And every day, he grew more alarmed. He had thought the Germans were a little out of their minds, with the way they followed that lunatic Hitler and everything, but the Japs just sounded out and out crazy. His nightmares, which since coming on board had reverted to his torpedo version, were slowly changing from a fanatical German to a drugged-up, suicidal, Japanese crew trying their best to kill him. He was in the middle of a nightmare about a torpedo when alarms began sounding. Henry hit the floor and screamed, "They got us! They got us, the damned bastards." When he realized where he was and noticed the shocked expressions of his crew, he stood up and smiled. "Sorry about that," he said sheepishly. Further explanation was unnecessary, as the loud speaker called for their attention.

"Two atomic bombs were dropped on Japan and the Imperial Japanese armed forces have surrendered unconditionally." The voice cracked. Shouts went up all over the ship. Henry heard men arguing about the atomic bombs. He knew exactly what they were: the miracles that he had been praying for. He lay back down, and for the first time since boot camp, he slept a dreamless night.

Chapter Ten

Doris was standing at the train station with Katy and the rest of the family, awaiting Billy's train. She was just as happy as anyone that the war was over, but she was tired of the hugs and attempted kisses. It seemed that she and Katy had to ward of hundreds of kisses in the last few weeks. She suspected that the military boys were using the war's end as an excuse. LW Sr. had gotten a laugh out of her observation.

"Why, Doris, you have to allow some stowed up tension to be let loose. Why, there's some now," he said as he bent over to plant a big kiss on her cheek. She screamed and tried half-heartedly to push him away. Luckily, her mother-in-law came to her rescue and pulled the would-be offender away.

A train whistle could be clearly heard in the distance. Both Katy and Doris had tears welling up in their eyes. LW Sr. had a beer in one hand and his wife in the other. Billy stepped off the train in full uniform, with medals hanging off his chest. Katy ran quickly into his arms and held on tight. Doris could wait no longer, and she ran and threw her arms around both of them.

"My God, I can read the headlines now: boy survives the horror of war only to be smothered by the horror at home," LW Sr. said with a laugh. His wife slapped him and then went and joined the other women who were attempting to get to the young hero. Billy finally freed himself and went over to greet the men. His father wrapped him in a bear hug while the rest of the men patted him on the back and offered beer. Katy stayed right with him like she was afraid she would lose him again. As he shook hands with LW Sr., he asked, "Have you heard from LW?"

"Not for a month or so."

"Well I am sure he will be home soon."

Katy and Billy were married the next month. Henry arrived home one week after the wedding. He had tried to get a hold of Tabby, but he had not gotten a response. He smiled as his eyes fell on Billy and his new bride.

"I can't believe that you fooled her into marrying you."

"Well it is too late now," Billy replied.

"I am so sorry," Henry said as he gave a big hug to Katy.

"Well I'm not," Katy stated.

"Then you sure don't know him very well," laughed Henry.

"I bet I know him better than you."

"Okay, you win." Henry gave up. His face took on a serious look. "Any word from LW?"

"Not one, and it's been a while," Billy replied sadly. An awkward silence engulfed the group as Doris and LW's mom and dad walked up.

"How are you?" Doris asked with a smile.

"Well, Doris, don't you look stunning."

"Why, thank you, Henry. And you look so handsome in your uniform."

A disturbance broke out behind them. LW Sr. had tripped, knocking a young woman into another man, and then LW Sr. finished it off by taking out a trash can. Red-faced and cussing up a storm, he managed to get to his feet. One look from his wife was enough to silence him. Doris started laughing, and the rest of the group followed suit.

Katy looked at Doris strangely and then said, "You've heard from LW?"

Doris smiled mischievously. "What makes you think that?"

"You wouldn't have that glint in your eye if you hadn't."

"Come on, Doris, don't keep us in suspense," Billy cried.

"Oh, okay. I got a letter saying his ship was headed home."

"When?" asked Henry.

"He wasn't clear on the date, but he said we should expect him to arrive here within six weeks." Now everyone became excited. All three had served their country, and soon they would all be safe at home.

*****

Within hours of the carrier *Bella Wood's* arrival in port, LW had filled out all the paperwork needed for his dismissal from the navy. He sent a letter home and then found a place to bed down. He was surprised at the speed of his release. Within a week, LW found himself out of the navy and in the navy reserve. He purchased a ticket and caught the first available train home. He found a window seat and settled in. The train was full of sailors and soldiers returning home; it was also full of wives and girlfriends. Four girls dressed in slacks sat behind him; the red crosses on their sleeves announced them as nurses. Moments after the train started rolling, LW began to doze off. Suddenly, something woke him, he couldn't put his finger on it; he thought he had heard a familiar name. The four nurses behind him were telling war stories. He turned his head and put his ear in the crack between the seats.

"So we are walking along this trail overlooking the beach when he turns and starts to kiss me."

"Did you let him?" one of the nurses asked.

"I did, and when he finished, I stepped back and said, 'Henry, I'm not that kinda girl.'"

"You didn't really say that!" one of them said, putting her hands to her mouth.

"Yes, I did, and he turned three shades of red."

"How could you do that to him?"

"I was just having a little fun. Then, after he had suffered enough, I kissed him!" They all started laughing.

"What happened to him?"

"In the last letter I received, he said he was heading home."

"Where is home?" they inquired.

"He is from Fort Worth."

"A Texas boy. Well good for you."

"Does he know you're coming?"

"No, I thought I would surprise him."

"He probably lives on ranch, and his dad has lots of money."

"What did you say his name was?"

"Henry, Henry Hartman." The girls were interrupted by loud laughs from the seat in front of them.

"He is just the most caring, thoughtful, and sweetest guy I've ever known," Tabby said, trying to ignore the rude sailor. This time, the roaring laughter could not be ignored. Tabby leaned over and found herself looking down at a young pilot with tears rolling down his face.

"Just what is your problem? Didn't your mother teach you not to eavesdrop on other people's conversations?" she said testily.

"Henry, Henry Hartman—sweet! Haha!" LW screamed.

"How would you know? Wait a minute, do you know him?" she asked.

"Henry, caring and thoughtful! Haha! It's too much."

Seeing that she was being completely ignored, Tabby's nursing instincts took over. She reached down and pinched LW under his arm.

"Now answer me. Do you know Henry?"

LW was squealing in pain, and his desire to hit a girl had never been stronger. Finally, he managed to get an answer out. "Yes, I know him."

Tabby grew excited. "How do you know him?"

LW remembered his training and said, "Loose lips sink ships."

"The only ship that's going to sink around here is you, sailor, if you don't start talking."

"Okay, I was just having some fun. Henry is my cousin."

Tabby moved into the aisle and asked the soldier sitting next to LW if he would trade seats with her. He looked at her and then back at her now empty seat and the three wary nurses, and readily agreed. Tabby slid in next to LW and continued her interrogations.

"How do I know that you are really his cousin? Or that you even know him at all?"

"You don't. Now leave me alone," LW replied sharply.

She was about to respond when she remembered that Henry had a cousin who was a pilot in the navy. He had talked about him constantly;

his name was LW. Her excitement grew. "Okay, I'll leave you alone if you will answer me one question."

"What?" he replied irritably.

"Give me your name."

"That's not a question"

"Okay, what is your name"

"LW," he said.

"So you are Henry's cousin."

"I am glad we can both agree."

Tabby could not believe her good fortune. She had been trying to figure out how to find Henry. She had his address, so she figured on taking a cab. This would work out much better than she had hoped, and now she had someone with whom to talk about Henry.

LW could not believe his good fortune. He was facing a long, lonely ride home. Now he could bad-mouth Henry and have a pretty girl paying attention to him, too.

"So how did you meet Henry?" LW asked

"He was brought into our hospital in North Africa."

"I heard a little about that. He was blown up while he was going the bathroom outside his tank, right?"

"What? No, he was wounded trying to save his tank," she said.

"Who told you that, Henry?"

"Well, yes, I guess so."

"That figures. I think there's something's you should know about Henry."

"What about him?"

"He ... no I shouldn't say anything."

"Tell me."

"He exaggerates things. Like when we were little, he would always boast about how great a fisherman he was or the size of the fish he caught. It was always something. You take that tank ... he was outside, caught with his pants down. Yet he turns around and says he was saving his tank. Typical, typical Henry. Now I remember the time we were fishing and poor Billy had a big bass on the hook. Now he and that bass were in a serious fight. Billy was working that line like a magician. I was standing right there behind him, shouting and just rooting him on. And old Henry was laying out on a big limb just mouthing off and making fun of Billy. It was a terrible thing to hear. Always with the dirty words and causing trouble. Well, me and Billy had had enough, so we went over and jumped on that limb till it broke, and Henry fell right in the river."

"Well, good for you. I can't believe he would act that way," Tabby said sadly. LW didn't even notice the sadness in her voice. He was on a roll.

"That's what Cindy, his first wife, thought, too. She was always trying to help him, you know, with his drinking problem."

Tabby was aghast. She really didn't know Henry at all. By the time the train pulled into the station a day and a half later, Tabby knew she had made a mistake. She told LW what she thought and that she was heading home. She thanked him for saving her from a big mistake. LW was appalled. She had to get off and see Henry; otherwise his whole story was just a waste of time.

"No, you have to face Henry. Otherwise he will never know that you know the truth. He will have won, and you can't live like that."

"You're right, LW. I do need to face him."

"Okay, you wait here, and I will go and greet my family. Afterward, I will come and get you. That way, you can catch Henry off guard." She was so angry with Henry that she couldn't wait to see him, so she agreed to LW's plan.

*****

The entire family was once again waiting on the platform for the safe return of the last of their sons. Doris was standing in front with LW's parents. Henry was standing right behind her. As the train pulled up, he leaned down and whispered in Doris's ear.

"I sure hope they were able to cure whatever it was that LW caught from all those Asian women."

"What are you talking about, Henry?"

"You know. I am sure LW told you about it."

"He did not tell me anything of the sort."

"I am sorry. I may have spoken out of turn."

The train came to a stop and people began filing off. Soldiers and sailors were suddenly everywhere. In the confusion, LW was able to move within a few feet of his family before he was spotted. Doris jumped into his arms and locked on for dear life. His mother soon joined her. The two females almost overpowered him. His father, beaming from ear to ear, shoved his big hand in the pile and came out with his son. Next, LW turned and greeted Henry and Bill. Henry had a mischievous grin on his face, and LW grinned back, each oozing with anticipation for the springing of the trap he had set. Doris looked in his eyes and then said, "Let's go home. You have something to tell me, I believe."

"What? Oh yes, I have a lot to tell you," LW said, slightly confused.

"I'll bet you do," Henry stated with a knowing smile.

LW felt alarm bells going off but he was too busy thinking of Tabby to pay much attention to them.

"Henry, I almost forgot; I found something of yours."

Now it was Henry's turn to be confused as he watched his cousin jump back up into the train.

"Now what's that all about?" Henry asked out loud.

"I don't know, but it can't be good. Watch yourself," Billy warned. His worry was increasing every second. There was no telling what his cousin had brought for them. Images of body parts instantly came to mind but were dismissed due to searches done by the military. Still, a vast amount of stolen items were making their way back to the States. Just then, their cousin emerged from the train, holding hands with a beautiful young girl. Billy was astounded; this was not what he was expecting. He saw Doris flash by and watched as she stormed up to LW.

"So this is why you haven't written! Does she know that you're married," Doris demanded.

"Of course she does," LW replied.

Doris was flabbergasted. She had no idea what to say. And to make matters worse, LW wasn't even paying attention to her. He was smiling and looking back over her head. She began to feel faint. LW, for his part, was so engrossed with watching Henry that he had completely forgotten about Doris. Doris felt her knees start to buckle, when Henry rudely pushed by her and stepped up to the young and obviously frightened girl. At the sight of Henry, her face went from frightened to angry. Henry stared at her and finally said, "Hello, Tabby. How on earth did you get here?"

"I came to see you, Henry. I wanted to tell you how much I care for you and that I didn't want to live without you."

Henry was overwhelmed. The love of his life had just magically appeared before his eyes. She was even more lovely than he remembered. He was speechless, barely hearing what she was saying to him.

"I was all set to come find you, when lo and behold, I run into your cousin, to whom I owe a huge debt. We spent the entire train ride from San Diego talking about you, the real you. Where's Cindy? Did you leave her at home with your second wife and all your kids?"

LW backed slowly away. His work was done, and there was no sense in getting caught up in this lovers' spat. He caught a dazed Doris by the hand and led her to his waiting parents. "Let's go home."

He looked over to a wide-eyed Billy and said, "It's sure good to be home. Things haven't changed a bit."

Billy stared with his mouth open as his cousin got in the car and drove away. He turned and looked back at Henry.

"LW said you would act surprised and the deny all of it. I can't believe how many nights I wasted on you, dreaming of the day we would be back together."

Henry was still trying to absorb the fact that his dream had materialized. "Didn't want to live without me; what is that supposed to mean? And did you say the whole trip with LW?" Realization hit home and hit home hard. He had just been one-upped. "LW told you I was a liar; he told you I was married."

"Twice. You have been married twice and have two children."

"What? I have never been married and sure don't have any kids."

"He told me you would say that."

"Of course he said I would say that, because it's true. You can't believe LW; he is full of—"

"Don't you say it. I just spent the last two days sitting right next to him on a train. He was extremely thoughtful and kind. And I won't stand here and let you tear him down."

"Well if you don't want to believe me, then ask my cousin here," he said, turning to Billy, who was laughing at the brilliant set up. Henry was caught off guard twice. Once when the girl stepped off the train, and then again when she unloaded on him. LW had obviously not lost his touch and flair.

So when his cousin turned to him for support, Billy himself was caught off guard. Before he could answer, Tabby threw a stab at him. "So you're the infamous Billy. Let me guess, Henry has never been married and doesn't have any children. And he didn't make fun of you while you were fighting a fish in the river. And you and LW didn't jump on a limb until it broke." She stood eyeing him critically with her hand on her hip.

Billy was so shocked at the depth of LW's treachery that he simply could not respond. "Um … um … well you, um, see …"

"LW said you both were just as bad as the other."

Henry finally realized how well his cousin had laid his trap. He thought about turning to his parents, but LW would have covered that as well. The only one who could prove him true was Doris, and LW had escaped with her. They were all supposed to meet at LW's for a welcome home party. If he could convince her to go with him, then he could get Doris to vouch for him. He mentioned this to her, and she shot fire bolts out of her eyes.

"Do you really think I am going to go to a house full of people who know how you are and let you make a fool of me again?" Now he was beaten. Without Doris, he was finished.

His salvation came in the form of a slender girl with a pony tail. Katy had stood unnoticed behind Billy. She liked Henry and knew all three of the boys well. She had no doubts about what was happening. She stepped up beside Henry and looked Tabby in the eyes. "Hello, I am Katy Hartman, Billy's wife. So you are the one Henry has been so lovesick over. It's a pleasure to finally meet you." Despite her anger, Tabby took the outstretched hand. Katy continued. "How about me? Did LW say anything bad about me?"

Billy's head came up at the thought of someone saying something bad about his wife. "No. As a matter of fact, he never mentioned Billy being married."

"That figures. He probably didn't know we were married and therefore he didn't foresee my attendance on the platform today. You see, I have known all three of them from way back in grade school. And I can assure you that Henry has never been married and has never had any children. I can also assure you that LW is full of … and Henry is one of the sweetest guys I know. He is also in love with you. Now unless you want to throw that away over some prank, I suggest we get in the car and go confront LW."

Tabby, looking back and forth between them with tears running down her cheeks, agreed. Henry let out the breath he was holding and went to give her a hug. She pushed him away. "Not yet."

"Yes, we will wait until after we confront LW," Henry said with a smile.

Katy noticed the tone and the sadistic smile. "Now, Henry, LW just got home, and you will not start anything. The same goes for you, Billy. And besides, I am sure you two have done something to welcome him home, as well." Both Henry and Billy's eyes fell. "Just as I thought. What did you boys do?" she demanded. Neither choose to answer. "Now we are going to need his and Doris's help if you want to make Tabby trust you."

Henry finally answered, "We told Doris that LW had caught a disease from all the Asian girls he was with."

Katy and Tabby both started to laugh. "You see what you have stepped into? You have to be on your guard around these three and take everything you hear with a grain of salt."

"I will keep that in mind," Tabby said, smiling at Katy. Henry felt relief rush through him and flashed a grateful smile at Katy.

*****

LW found himself swarmed by well-wishers with offers of food and drink. Doris stood quietly at his side, smiling and laughing. LW grew more concerned by the minute. Finally, they found a semi-quiet corner where they could converse.

"What is it that you wanted to tell me?" asked Doris sweetly. With a look of confusion on his face, LW struggled to make sense of the situation.

"I don't know what you're talking about."

"I think you do. If you tell the truth, I will be far more understanding."

"I really don't know what your talking about." Now he was growing uneasy, frantically flipping through his memories, looking for anything that could incriminate him. One incident after another came forward, and each was discarded. Many were embarrassing, some outright disgraceful, but none could draw this kind of attention from Doris. "Look, I really don't have a clue. If I have been accused of something, then at least allow me the ability to deny it," LW said desperately. His homecoming was not working out like he had planned.

"You mean you don't think I will notice or you don't care if I catch it?" She was beginning to get angry.

"Catch what? I don't have anything to catch."

"Just because the navy got rid of it doesn't make it all right."

"What are you talking about? Did you receive a medical report? What did it say I have? Where is it?" Now he was really desperate. Evidently, the navy had found something wrong with him.

"So you admit it then?" Doris said

"Would you please tell me what they said?" LW was pleading, visions of terrible tropical diseases flashing before him.

"They said you caught something from all those Asian girls you were with."

"The navy said that! There must be some mistake, a mix up of some kind." He breathed a sigh of relief.

"There's no mix up. You have been caught red-handed."

"Caught? Caught? You have to do something to get caught."

"So you're telling me you were never with anyone else?"

"Yes, that's exactly what I am saying. Most of the islands we stopped at were destroyed. The rest of the time, I was on board the carrier. I can't believe the navy sent a letter like that."

"You're telling me that you didn't catch a disease from some girl? Why would Henry and Bill say something like that?"

The truth behind what she had just asked set in. "Why would they say something like that? They lied to me!" She was beginning to grow angry.

LW was already there. The minute he heard Henry's name, he knew he had been set up.

"I am so sorry, LW. I should have known better." She felt like she had betrayed her marriage.

"That's okay. You couldn't have known." He was only half paying attention to her, his eyes seeking out the architect of this tall tale.

Henry and company had made a quick search of the house, and after not finding LW anywhere within its walls, they proceeded out into the backyard. After scouring the sea of heads, Henry spotted LW and Doris near the back fence. Evidently, they had just worked out the truth, for LW was turning away from Doris and his eyes were searching the crowd. Henry had little doubt that LW had deduced his deception and was seeking revenge. He would gladly give him satisfaction.

"Now remember, when we find him, we question him together. Henry, you aren't to do anything rash," Katy said. Then she watched as Henry vaulted the rails on the back porch and began pushing his way into the horde. She looked in the direction he was headed and spotted another figure forcing his way toward Henry. She yelled at Henry, but he ignored her. She looked around in desperation. Finally, she saw Billy calmly drinking a beer and leaning against a post.

"Billy, do something."

"Like what?"

"Stop Henry."

"Not a chance. Nothing can stop him, except maybe LW."

"You can't let them fight."

"No, you've got that backwards. I can't stop them, but I can let them fight." *Girls*, thought Billy. There was no way he was going to step in the middle of his two enraged cousins. He knew all too well that any interference on his part would be misconstrued. The combatants would, in all likelihood, turn on him. Besides, he had a great location to safely observe the fight.

LW and Henry collided without a word being spoken. They had each put on weight and learned a great deal while they were away. Henry could not believe the strength and speed of his opponent. Fists hit him from every direction, stunning in their speed and velocity.

LW, for his part, was impressed with ferocity of Henry's attack. His ability to block the blows he was throwing was also impressive. Maybe one out of five had landed, and most of those seemed to be ineffective. Clearly Henry was not the fighter LW remembered.

The crowd watched with a mixture of awe and disgust. Doris and Katy were both angry and seemed to care less about the fight that was quickly destroying the backyard. Tabby was shocked and appalled. LW and Henry's parents had made their way to the porch and stood staring at the bloody battle. Tabby screamed for someone to stop them.

"It's better just to let them fight it out," LW's mother said, remembering how her husband had always reacted to the boys' fights before.

LW's father was stunned by the brutality on display before him. These two were not the same boys who had fought so many times before. Fresh from the military and honed by the fires of war, they were trained not at fighting but at killing. He raced in to stop it before more permanent damage was done. "My God, they're going to kill each other," he bellowed. He and Henry's father tried their best to separate them. It was like trying to separate two slippery pieces of iron. Billy had slipped into the careless attitude that soldiers in battle often had. He was indifferent to the melee in front of him. Only when LW Sr. took a shot to the eye did he interfere. He ran up an tackled Henry from behind. The force of his blow drove Henry into the ground, and before he had time to recover, Billy had pinned his arms down behind his back. Five men grabbed LW and finally overcame him with sheer numbers.

LW Sr. slowly regained his feet and then walked back over to the two panting warriors. "Let's get something straight. You two aren't little boys. You're men. What's more, you're both trained to kill. Nothing you can do will reverse that training. So from now on, you will treat each other with respect. You will also remember that you are family, and family doesn't hurt each other. Now shake hands and apologize." Reluctantly, both of them shook hands and staggered towards the house. Doris ran out and helped LW to a chair. His mother walked out with towels and warm water. Tabby, who had seen soldiers fight many times before, moved in to examine the wounds. Doris fawned over LW for the rest of the day. His mother joined her, and LW loved every minute of it.

*****

Doris's parents announced that they were building a new house on the lot next to them and Doris and LW could live in their old house.

They both grew excited until LW Sr. reminded them that they would be living next door to Doris's mother. With that morbid fact bouncing around in his head, LW got in the car and headed out for some fishing with Billy. He stopped off at Billy's house to pick him up. Billy and Katy had bought a nice house and were in the process of getting it ready to move in. LW laughed as he kissed Katy good-bye and jumped into the car.

"Becoming the regular family man, aren't you?"

"Don't you just know it," Bill said, smiling.

"Well, I sure wish Henry was going with us. I can't understand him running off with that girl. He barely knows her."

"He is in love. Besides, they spent a lot of time together in the hospital. During the war, it didn't take long to get to know someone. You should know that, LW."

"Yep, I sure do." LW popped open a beer. He grew sad as he thought about Archie. His mind kind of drifted off, and Billy gave him with a knowing look. After a while, Billy cleared his throat.

"You know, everyone sort of lost touch with you for a few months." LW didn't say anything for a moment. Billy reached for another beer and patiently waited for his reply. LW sighed and then began to talk.

"There was a friend of mine named Archie. He was a pilot, too. We became real close. Not like Henry and Tabby, mind you." He gave a searching look at Billy, waiting for the sarcastic remarks that might come. Satisfied that his cousin wasn't reading anything more into it, he continued, "Well, we flew together on quite a few missions. Matter of fact, he shot the hell out of me on one of them." This revelation caught Billy off guard. Soldiers often bitterly cursed the navy pilots who ripped through American platoons. It was hard enough to watch men die; it was harder still to watch as your own planes gunned them down. The fact that they could shoot each other had never crossed his mind.

"Anyway, we had gotten close, as I was telling you. One day we were on the tail end of a patrol when Archie spotted a big fat Jap plane flying like he was on a Sunday drive. We dove and took him out. All the sudden, I felt my plane taking hits, and then Archie's plane just disintegrated. I watched as he fell into the sea."

Billy was no stranger to friends suddenly blowing apart. He had seen many a man suffer the same fate. But soldiers died during attacks; they weren't blown out of the clear blue sky. He sensed that his cousin was not through. Reaching over, he gave him another beer and a quick grip on the shoulder.

They pulled up to the creek and got out. Neither one spoke a word while they got set up. As usual, LW went for the brim, and he smiled as he watched Billy rig up for a run at some catfish. After both corks were in the water, Billy leaned back and looked at LW.

"You were saying?" They sat in silence for several minutes before LW continued.

"After Archie went down, I lasted for a few more minutes." He shot a quick look at Billy. "I was outnumbered, and I gave better than I got. Then I was hit again, and I went down. Spent about an hour and a half in the water. Sea plane showed up to rescue me; that's when the shark came." Billy wasn't expecting that, and it was apparent. LW laughed at his expression and then went back to his story. "Big great white. Bastard bit my foot. Just seeing if he liked the taste, I guess. Anyway, now I know how a fish feels." Billy was thinking what it must have felt like to be bobbing in the open ocean like a cork, waiting for a shark to bite you. No wonder LW hadn't been the same. His thoughts were interrupted as his line began running. His rod was bent over and he heaved. Something heavy was on the other end of his line. Billy thought that the weight felt funny; he said as much to LW.

"That's cuz it's a turtle," LW said.

"Could be a big catfish," Billy replied without much enthusiasm.

"Nope it's a turtle"

Billy had to agree; it felt like a turtle. A few seconds later, a snapping turtle's head broke the surface. "Damn," Billy sighed as he cut the line. LW caught a small perch, and Billy snickered. He watched as LW rerigged and then harpooned the perch with his hook and quickly tossed him into the creek. Billy switched to worms in an attempt to avoid a repeat performance. LW's rod snapped down, and he pulled back to set the hook. Both men began howling when a largemouth bass broke the water. Billy grabbed the net while LW worked the bass closer to the shore. They were fishing in a relatively wide portion of the creek; it was perhaps fifteen feet deep and maybe twice that in width. So the fight was short-lived and the fish was quickly pulled to shore. Billy didn't have long to admire their catch; his line began running again. His heart sank as he felt the way his line was being pulled. Instead of a strong fight, he felt dead weight. He sighed; another turtle. Luckily, his partner was too busy to notice; his attention was centered on the bass and his stringer. A quick snap of the line and he was back in business. LW secured another perch, which he clearly envisioned as bait.

Billy threw his line in and sat back down, drinking his beer as he reflected on the differences between prewar and postwar LW. He was happy that his cousin had not seen the second turtle, yet at the same time, he was disturbed because the LW he knew would not only have seen it but would be rubbing it in. He sat contemplating this when LW's line began running again. This time, LW was not hollering; as a matter of fact, he seemed a bit put out. He was mumbling and jerking his rod. So intent was Billy on watching the progress of the line that he missed the sideways glance and the smile that would have sent shivers down his back had he seen it. With a huge tug, LW sent the black snake flying clear of the creek and headed straight as a bullet into Billy's lap. The courage that had been proven in countless battles withered in a flash. Billy screamed and rolled on the ground, kicking and slapping his way free. LW had thought it would be funny to bring the fish snake flying toward his cousin. Everything happened perfectly; Billy remained unaware at the true nature of the creature on the other end of the line. The same could be said about the nature of his cousin. The snake had been jerked out of the water with precision and timing. LW was already laughing when he saw the bright white of the snake's mouth. He tried to pull back, but it was useless. There was far too much line. Billy was on his back, kicking, while he clawed his way up the bank.

The cotton mouth, with venom dripping, came toward him as fast as possible, striking again and again, trying to sink those deadly fangs where they would do the most damage: Billy's soft flesh. It had struck repeatedly only to be met with the unyielding leather of the bottom of Billy's boot. Finally, Billy hit the bottom of a large tree; there was now nowhere else to run. The snake drew its head back for another strike. Suddenly, something huge drove the snake down into the dirt. It fought and wiggled and then felt an incredibly sharp pain. The weight on its neck eased and it felt itself kicked aside. As soon as the snake hit the ground, it tried to crawl back to the intended victim, only to find that it couldn't move. Flipping over, the snake looked down along his body only to see it end three inches away in a bloody stump. It lay glaring at the two creatures it hated most in the world.

LW threw down his useless rod and pulled out his pocket knife. He stepped on the neck of the snake, and with one quick motion, removed it's head. Billy stopped moving and stared up at his cousin. The worry on LW's face was almost comical. He gave Billy's feet and legs a thorough examination. Satisfied, he picked up his pole and cut the line. "I am very sorry, Billy. If I had known it was a cottonmouth, I would never have done that."

Still in shock, Billy stood up and walked over to the now severed head. The moment he got close to it, the eyes focused on him and the mouth opened. He kicked it hard into the brush. He noticed the fishing line still hooked in it's throat.

"Ain't much of fisherman that don't retrieve his hook," he said.

LW smiled. "Kinda like a man who loses two rigs to turtles."

Billy smiled; his cousin had seen both of his catches.

Chapter Eleven

Henry had returned home with a new bride. Both came over to help
LW and Doris move into their new four-bedroom, two-bath house. It
had a small kitchen and a large living room. Watching LW Sr. carry
objects that he couldn't see over was worth the work. He tripped and
fell constantly; this was usually followed by a tirade of cuss words.
His wife followed him with the apologies. Doris found all this to be
extremely funny.

LW had gone to work with the local newspaper, where his father
worked. LW Sr. was not the least bit happy about this development.
Not that he was against helping his son; he just wanted something
more for him.

Henry had gotten a job as a lineman with the electric company.
Billy had tried to make a go as a taxidermist, a passion of his since
childhood, but the money just wasn't there. Henry was trying to get
him on with him, but it was taking a while. Billy decided to take a job
with the water department in the meantime. He and Katy loved their
house and were anxious to start their family.

It did not take long to move LW and Doris's things in. When the
last items were put in their place, they served their family watermelon

on the front porch. Billy cleared his throat. "Excuse me, but I have announcement to make."

"Well, then by all means, proceed Mr. Proper," LW said sarcastically.

Billy ignored him. "Katy and I are pregnant."

Both Doris and Tabby clapped and then threw their arms around Katy. Henry and the guys vigorously shook Billy's hand and offered their congratulations. LW Sr. put his arm around Billy's neck. He pointed his free hand at LW and said, "You see, boy, that's why it's impossible to get rid of the Catholics. They reproduce like rabbits." Everyone laughed. Katy hung her head as she turned red from embarrassment.

That night, as they lay sleeping, Doris snuggled close to LW. "Do you think we could have one soon?"

"Have one what?" asked LW, half asleep.

"You know exactly what I'm talking about," she said shyly.

"No, I … good Lord, Doris, we're not Catholic," LW said.

"That's got nothing to do with it."

"My father was right; it is contagious."

"I doubt that. But let's hear his grand thought anyway."

"Well, Doris, if I didn't know any better, I would swear that you were mocking him."

"Spill it, fly boy."

"He said that in a few months, all three of you would be pregnant."

"Now why would he say something like that?"

"He said once one of you is expecting, the others will get all worked up until you're pregnant, too."

"I hope you didn't believe him."

"I wasn't sure until tonight, and then sure enough, you brought it up." He started laughing, and she hit him with her pillow. *Perhaps my father was right,* LW thought as he drifted off to sleep.

The next day, LW went outside to mow the yard. After he was through with the front yard, he felt a strange sensation like he was being watched. He looked up, and his mother-in-law was staring at him. He killed the motor, and she said, "What's wrong with you?"

"I'm sorry?" LW said, confused.

"I know that, but are you slow as well?"

"I'm sorry," he stated again

"We both agree on that, but it still doesn't excuse this racket so early in the morning."

"But it's after nine," he said defensively

"Much too early for that kind of racket. After you finish your yard, you can mow ours." With that, she turned and walked back into the house. LW was astounded. How he was going to hold his tongue day after day was beyond him. It took him an hour and a half to finish both lawns.

He had just finished putting up his equipment when he heard a car pull up in the driveway. His father's voice traveled perfectly in the clear morning air. He was telling his wife about a baseball game he had heard on the radio. LW smiled and walked out front. His parents were carrying groceries up the front steps. "I told ya'll we can make it. You don't have to bring us food." He quickly moved to help his mother.

"If I choose to bring my son food, I will do so. Nobody is going to tell me what I can or can't do," she said in a tone that left little to debate. As soon as he heard this, LW Sr. sped into the house. Doris came out from a back room to see what all the fuss was about.

"Hello, darling. You look stunning this morning," LW Sr. said as he planted a big kiss on her cheek.

"This is such a nice gesture, but you really don't need to do this," Doris said as she greeted her mother-in-law.

"Now don't you start, too. I simply won't hear it. LW, the Fourth of July is coming up, and we have been talking about going to the coast." The way she said it was both inviting and commanding.

"That's a long drive. If we drove up on Saturday, we would only have one day before we had to come home," LW stated.

"That's why we will leave Friday morning, enjoy two days at the beach, and then come home sometime Monday." She barely looked up as she answered him.

"I don't know if I can take off Friday. I would have to ask tomorrow. It's kind of short notice."

"That's why your father already requested it, for both of you." She was extremely pleased with herself.

"Of course, if you would rather stay and work, we'll understand."

He had been set up. The only question was how deep the conspiracy went. "Billy, Katy, Henry, and Tabby will be joining us. Doris, did your parents give you an answer yet?" his mother asked sweetly. He now knew just how deep the roots of betrayal ran.

"Yes. They regret that they have other plans," Doris said, not looking her husband in the eyes.

LW Sr. smiled and said, "Well, it's all settled then; we're going to the coast."

*****

Three cars loaded to capacity headed south. LW was sitting in the back seat with Doris. He had a toothpick in his mouth, and his feet were sticking dangerously out the window. They could hear his parents talking, but with all four windows down, it was impossible to carry on a conversation. Doris was already asleep, so with a satisfied smile on his lips, he slowly closed his eyes.

Soon, he woke with a start. He had no idea what had awoken him, but he narrowed it down to two possibilities. The first was the squealing of the tires followed by the violent movement of the car; the second was the cussing and screaming coming from the front seat. He glanced over at his wife and could not believe that she was able to sleep through this. The car twisted and turned and finally came to a stop. His mother began pounding on her husband. LW looked at Doris and saw that she was no longer asleep. She was staring straight ahead and barely breathing, clearly in shock.

"What was that all about?" LW asked sharply.

"He fell asleep, that's what happened," his mother shouted.

"No I did not! There was a deer in the road!" LW Sr. said defensively. The more he thought about it, the better he liked it. "What did you want me to do, hit the deer?" he demanded.

"That's a lie. You were asleep. If your daughter-in-law hadn't screamed, we would all be dead now," his wife said accusingly.

Surprised, LW looked over at Doris and realized she had been awake through out the entire ordeal. It had been her scream that had first awoken him.

"I'm telling you, there was a deer," he said stubbornly.

His wife looked back at Doris and asked, "What did you scream about?"

"Well, I awoke and thought that everyone else was asleep. I could be wrong," she said hesitantly.

"You know what you saw," her mother-in-law said.

Just then, Billy came running up to the car. "Are ya'll alright? What happened?"

"A deer ran out in front of us," LW Sr. said quickly.

"One of those invisible deer," his wife replied acidly. Billy realized he had walked into an argument and decided that discretion followed by retreat was the best strategy. LW Sr. started the engine and drove slowly out of the ditch. They continued their nine-hour drive. Curiously, no one felt much like sleeping.

LW tasted a strange flavor in the air. Memories flooded back, and he knew they were close to the coast. A full five minutes later, Doris made it known that she could taste the salt air. They then came around a bend in the road, and as far as the eye could see, farm fields stretched in every direction. About five miles farther, they spotted a small farm house sitting alongside a creek. There were clothes on the line and chickens scratching in the yard. A small sign written carefully on a board proclaimed that this house was selling fresh produce.

"Let's stop and buy some fruit," Annie said.

"You won't hear any complaints from me," LW Sr. replied. He had spotted watermelons. LW watched as Doris and the rest of his party converged on the farmer's goods. He walked slowly towards the creek and noticed a young boy fishing. The boy had a limb from a tree as a fishing pole. Line was tied around the end, and a homemade cork bobbed up and down. It dropped suddenly and they reemerged, only to disappear again. The boy gave a yank and then lifted a perch from the water. He dropped the fish in a bucket and then slid a grasshopper on his hook. LW noticed that his bucket was full of small perch. Watching the boy fish seemed to relax him, and he barely noticed as Doris walked up beside him. She gently put her hand in his and joined his quiet observance of the boy and his creek. She handed LW a peach as the boy landed another fish. He bit into the fruit, tasted its sweetness, and felt its cool, sticky fluid flow down his chin. Doris smiled and gently wiped it off. Their respite was interrupted by his father's booming voice. They piled back into the cars, now loaded with fresh fruits and vegetables, and continued their odyssey

Thirty minutes later, they spotted another roadside stand. This one lacked a house and the variety of the fruit stand. It sold tacos and boasted two choices: with or without hot sauce. You could also buy Mexican colas or beer.

"You would think with these choices, we would be in Mexico," LW Sr. grumbled.

"Well, we are closer to Mexico than to the boarder of any other state," Doris pointed out.

LW bit into his taco and grunted. "Dang, these things are good."

"I don't think they're worth ten cents apiece," LW Sr. replied.

"Don't mock them until you have tried one, Dad," LW retorted. It sounded garbled as he continued to stuff the newly discovered delicacy into his already dangerously full mouth.

"Don't talk with your mouth full, dear," his mother said.

"Damn, these things are good," LW Sr. stated after finally taking a bite.

"You could make a killing selling these things back home," LW said. As they finished eating, the ocean broke out before their eyes.

"I can't get used to seeing the water just appear like that. It's almost the same level as the land. Someday, that water is just going to spill out and flood all the way to San Antonio," LW Sr. observed. They kept one eye on the water and the other looking for signs to direct them to Port Aransas.

*****

When they arrived at the beach house they had rented for the weekend, everyone ran for the water—everyone except LW and his parents. His father moved out in search of the key, and his mother stood watching her son.

"Don't you want to join in on the fun?" she asked.

"No, I think I want to unload the car and get cleaned up." She watched him carry suitcases up the stairs with a concerned look upon her face. The beach house was built on stilts; the house itself was about eight feet off the ground. Piers extended from the sand to the floor, making a strange kinda of garage. Tools and fishing equipment were hung here and there, with car parts and other items scattered among them.

The harder LW Sr. looked, the more mazelike his surroundings began to appear. What had seemed like easy instructions three days ago were now beginning to seem like a puzzle created by a madman. Six piers from the stairs and then three piers to the left—that's what the rental agent had said. It had seemed easy; he had even cut the agent off as he tried to repeat it. He wished he had asked for more specific instructions. Six piers from the stairs, that was simple, or so you would think. The stairs ran parallel to the house, so which part of the stairs would you start counting from? He knew it was hanging behind some fishing gear, but there was fishing gear everywhere. He was getting more frustrated by the minute. He moved out to the center of the house and spun in a circle, spotting a cast net hanging from a rafter. He walked towards it and stepped into a metal bait bucket. Cursing, he fell forwards and tried to catch himself on the cast net, succeeding only in pulling it down on top of him and actually accelerating his fall. That's how his wife and son found him: one foot in a bucket and wrapped from his waist up in a net. They could not contain their laughter. LW leaned against a pier and noticed four or five old reels hanging from a nail.

"What are you doing?" his wife asked.

"Looking for the damn keys!" he exclaimed. "I am going to strangle that rental agent."

"Where did he say the keys were?" she asked

"Six piers from the stairs and three over, behind some fishing gear."

LW looked at the reels and then pushed them aside. Two keys on a chain were hanging from the same nail. Smiling, LW jingled the keys "I can see how they would be hard to find."

His father had managed to free himself and glared menacingly at his son. LW walked away laughing.

"You shouldn't feel bad. If you hadn't fallen so close to them, he would not have found them either."

"That's true. I would have already found them if I hadn't slipped on this bucket. What kinda moron leaves a bucket in the middle of the floor?"

"The same kinda moron who hangs his key so far back from the stairs. Can you imagine the problems we would have had trying to locate those things in the dark?" Annie said. She was really thinking of what kinda of damage her husband would have caused. By the time they got upstairs, Doris had returned and was standing on the balcony with LW.

*****

The next morning, the guys began fishing at sunup. Billy, Henry, and LW Sr. decided to try their luck in the surf. LW walked down the beach about a half a mile until he came to a small cut running back into the dunes. He placed a shrimp on the line and dropped it into the water. He felt an immediate tug on his line and jerked his rod up. His shrimp was cut in half, but other than that, his hook was empty. He dropped it back in and again felt a tug. This time, he slowly pulled the hook to the surface. He was rewarded by seeing a huge crab holding desperately to the shrimp. As soon as the crab saw him, it let go and fell back into the water. LW smiled and looked back toward the rest of the group. Let them try to catch enough fish to feed everybody; the girls would be far more impressed with his bounty. This time, when he felt a tug, he eased it to the surface and then quickly swung the crab over onto the sand. When the crab let go, he found himself exposed on dry land. LW kicked him upside down and lifted him into the bucket. After about thirty minutes, LW had filled his five-gallon bucket with blue crabs. He picked up his bucket and headed back to the beach house. As he got closer, he decided to cut through the dunes and avoid the guys. He made it to the house undetected and found an old ice chest to dump his crabs in. Locating another bucket, LW headed back to the cut. As he neared the guys, Billy looked up and said, "Gave up so soon?"

"No, I just needed another bucket to sit on. Any luck?"

"Your father caught a shark."

This caught LW's interest. "What kind?"

"Hammer head," his father replied.

"How big?"

"Just a baby, maybe sixteen inches." LW observed Henry fighting through the surf, trying to throw his line out farther.

"Are you sure you don't want to join us?" his father asked.

"Hell no. He wants to go sit alone and clean up on trout," Billy said sarcastically. This brought laughter from everyone, even LW.

"If I don't catch something soon, I will come get some advice. That is, if you don't mind putting up with a novice." With that, he turned and headed back to his spot. He made two more trips back to the cooler, completely filling it with crabs. After he dumped the last bucket in, he eyed the cast net. It looked simple enough. Picking it up, he headed back down the beach.

Doris had seen him carrying something and had gone to investigate. He heard her approaching but was too busy staring down his cousins. They saw him carrying a net and it was just too much for them.

"Gave up trying to catch them like a man?" Henry yelled.

LW just kept walking. Doris felt the need to defend her husband, though she it did it in typical female fashion.

"You boys catch anything?" They dropped their eyes in shame. "We are sure looking forward to some fresh seafood for dinner."

LW put his own head down and smiled. When they reached the cut, he got his fishing rod ready for her and then instructed her on how to catch them.

"If there are so many crabs, why haven't you kept them?" she questioned. She felt the tug and did as she was instructed. As she swung her catch onto the beach, she yelled, "That's hideous!" She then began screaming as the crab scurried back to the water. It came right for her, and she panicked. Luckily, her husband didn't, and right as the crab reached the water's edge LW flipped it upside down. He tossed it in the bucket and teased his wife about it. He was ready to try his cast net. He threw it ten times and could not get it right. On the eleventh try, the net opened half way before hitting the water. He was pleased to see five good-sized shrimp and some small fish. His next throw opened about the same, and this time it was full of shrimp. This was more like it. He continued to fill up his bucket of shrimp while helping Doris fill the other with crabs.

*****

They found the beach all but deserted when they returned. Only his father remained, sitting in a lawn chair wearing shorts and a sombrero that he had purchased at the grocery store.

"I can't believe he fell asleep," Doris said.

"More like passed out," LW replied. Their conversation was interrupted by voices coming from the deck.

"I wonder if LW caught anything," they heard Henry say.

"No better luck than us, I'll bet," Billy retorted

"You boys better hope not," Tabby piped in. LW put his finger to his lips and carried both buckets under the house. Doris watched as he pulled the ice chest out, straining with every step. He then escorted her up the steps and into the house. They washed up and made sandwiches. They were soon spotted by the rest of their party.

"Please tell me you caught something. I really don't want to have to pay for seafood tonight," his mother said desperately.

"Don't worry, Mom. We wouldn't let you down," LW stated with a deadpan expression.

"What did you catch?" Billy asked

Without a word, LW headed down the stairs. He was chewing on an apple as he causally lifted the lid and exposed the pile of crabs.

"Damn, where did you buy those?" Billy asked.

Ignoring her nephew, Annie put her arms around her son. "Well done, LW!"

LW turned and went under the house again. He returned with two buckets. Everyone looked at the buckets of shrimp in amazement. His mother ran upstairs and began getting out pans. LW found a lawn chair and began removing the heads from the shrimp. His cousins went in and found more chairs and joined him. It wasn't long before they had the shrimp ready for the pot.

"Start bringing up the crabs," LW's mother yelled. LW started up the stairs with the two buckets. He was followed closely by his cousins with the ice chest. They managed to make it all the way into the kitchen before they dropped it. When they dropped it, they didn't drop it straight but at an angle. The lid caught on a cabinet handle and popped open. To the horror of the girls and the delight of the guys, six crabs escaped and began crawling in different directions. It took them a few minutes to restore order. LW dumped the bucket into the boiling pans. The aroma of the crabs and the herbs soon filled the room. This process continued for about an hour. The girls set the table, and then they all sat down to enjoy their meal. LW looked over as his cousins sat down.

"What are you two doing?"

"We're going to eat crabs," Henry replied.

"You only get to eat what you catch," LW said, smiling. "Unless, of course, you want to admit that I am by far the better fisherman," he said smugly.

"Now, LW, you shouldn't boast," his mother said sweetly.

"Oh, dear Lord, where is your father"? Doris asked. She had just realized that she had not seen him all afternoon. Everyone looked at each other.

"He couldn't still be on the beach?" Henry exclaimed They jumped up and ran out on the deck. Sure enough, he was still sitting in his chair, hat pulled down, and sound asleep.

"He's got to be burned to a crisp," Annie said.

"I'll get him," said LW.

He ran down the steps and approached his father. The tide had begun to come in, and water rushed around the legs of the chair. Standing behind the chair, LW yelled, "We're sinking!" His father jumped up and tried to run. He was tangled in the chair, which in turn was stuck in the sand. He fell face first into the shallow water. LW looked down at him and said, "Did you hear me? It's time for dinner." He started to turn around when a thought appeared to come to him. "You weren't sleeping, were you?" Spitting and choking, his father vehemently denied the accusation.

"That wasn't very nice, LW," his mother said upon his return. They could hear his father cussing as he came up the stairs. When he burst into the room, all eyes turned towards him—and then slowly went down his bright red body and then back up again.

"My God, you look just like one of these crabs," Billy stated.

"I feel just like one of those crabs." He eased gently down into a chair. "How much did you have to pay for this food?"

LW cleared his throat. His mother smiled and then let her husband in on the fruits of his son's labor. "LW and Doris caught all this."

"What! Where did you catch it?" he inquired.

"Down the beach a ways," LW stated.

"We would have told you about it, but you were asleep," Doris said with a smile. He didn't try to argue; he was too busy eating shrimp and complaining about the pain.

*****

After dinner, the group headed down to the beach while LW Sr. received medical attention from his wife. Billy and Henry gathered wood as LW dug a hole. Before long, they had a fire going, and they formed a ring around it. Doris was extremely content; she had just enjoyed a first-class seafood dinner and was surrounded by the people she cared most about.

"We should go for a swim," Henry said. The girls agreed, but Billy just looked at LW.

"Okay, let's go," LW said.

Billy felt pride for his cousin swell in his breast. He knew how hard this had to be for LW. Coming face-to-face with a man-eater in his element, unable to defend himself adequately, would leave any sane man nervous about entering the water again. The more he thought about it, the more he agreed with this point of view. "Any sane man," he said to himself.

"Did you say something, Bill?" LW inquired.

"No, I was just thinking out loud."

LW stared at his cousin for a moment and then smiled. He stripped off his shirt and ran into the water. Billy watched him with a bemused look on his face. Whatever baggage LW was carrying seemed to be getting lighter. He laughed; they were all carrying baggage. It wasn't something you talked about, but it was there just the same. His thoughts shifted as he noticed something funny in the water. The outline of something big was just visible in the moonlight. He walked towards the water for a closer look. Whatever it was, it was moving slow. He called out and pointed in its direction. To his horror, LW swam towards it. The thing kept coming, totally oblivious to their presence. LW was now about twenty feet from it when recognition set in.

"It's a turtle. A giant one," LW yelled.

Just then, another form appeared in the water. Then another. Soon, up and down the beach, round, dark forms could be spotted fighting the surf, slowly making their way onto the beach. The first one came out almost at Billy's feet and began crawling up the beach, towards the dunes. Everyone exited the water. Some wanted to get a better look at this odd convoy; others didn't want to be out in the dark surf that could hide such monsters. It was an awesome sight. As far as one could see, huge turtles were making their ponderous way into the dunes.

"What are they doing?" LW asked.

"I don't know," Billy replied. LW called for his parents to come out and see this. His father stared wide-eyed at the giant turtles.

"You could eat for a week on one of these things."

"You would think like that," his wife chided.

Billy followed one into the dunes and watched bewildered as it dug a hole. He sat watching long after the others had gone upstairs and found their respective beds. His patience was rewarded when the turtle began laying eggs. Though he had suspected this outcome, it was a relief to know for sure.

*****

LW awoke with a start. It was pitch black, and everyone was still asleep. He eased up and looked at the clock; it read four thirty. He quietly got dressed and headed out the door. The moon had long since made its path over the horizon, but the light from the stars seemed almost as bright. It was still cool, and the breeze felt great. LW had his fishing rod in hand, and he was headed for his small cut. When he arrived, he was surprised by the current in the water. It was obvious that the tide was on its way out. He walked towards the dunes with the intention of casting up the cut and allowing his shrimp to float down the current. Any remnant of sleep that remained in his head was instantly cleared when he heard the distinct buzz of an upset rattlesnake. LW took a few quick steps backward and then decided to fish the mouth of the cut, at least until sunup. His first cast landed about thirty yards into the surf. He worked it back and felt nothing. After a few more casts, he gave up and switched to a gold spoon. He flung it into the surf and managed to get it back about halfway before his rod was bent double. He fought the fish for a good four minutes before landing it. It was beautiful redfish, maybe thirty-six inches long. He dropped it in his bucket, which was far too small for it, and cast out again. This time, he only made it a quarter of the way before he hooked another. Deciding that his bucket could take no more, LW headed back for the house.

Upon arrival, his conscience got the best of him. He went upstairs to wake his father. It took about five minutes to wake the other three men. Not one of them actually believed him, but after yesterday's performance, they could not take any chances. And when they saw what LW was putting in the cooler, they ran to get their rods.

Billy started up the dune, thinking of fishing upstream and allowing his bait to flow down to the surf. LW saw his cousin heading in the same direction that he himself had earlier.

"I wouldn't go up there. There is a rattler up in those weeds," he warned. Billy smiled and started up the dune once more. LW Sr. looked at his son and then decided to fish in the surf. LW ignored Billy and cast out. He was rewarded by yet another redfish. This got the group excited, and everyone worked feverishly to get their lines rigged up. His father put on a silver spoon, cast out, and was shocked when his line snapped tight. He fought to reel the fish in, and finally it revealed itself: a speckled trout. Now everyone started reeling in fish—everyone except Billy. He was too busy trying to fend off the snakes. After a few moments, he finally had the upper hand. He flipped over one snake and glided past another; he then retreated back down to the beach. He arrived to find an ice chest packed full of fish. Billy avoided LW's eyes and moved up to join the harvest.

By sunup, they had filled two ice chests and three buckets with fish. The frenzy did not end until after eight o'clock. They spent the next hour cleaning fish. LW's mother was astonished by the amount of meat they had cleaned. She knew they could not possibly eat all of it, so she ordered LW to get sacks and ice. All three of the younger couples piled into one car and headed for town.

"We need to find some fireworks," LW stated.

"Yes, we do," Billy seconded.

"Not until after we get the supplies your mother asked for," Doris said, knowing how easily the men could be distracted.

"Why don't you guys drop us off and then go look for fireworks?" Katy said.

As soon as they hit the outskirts of the little town, they spotted a store selling fireworks.

"I think we will take the car and come pick you guys up after we get through shopping," Doris stated.

"Sounds good," LW said, barely hearing his wife. Normally he would have thrown a fit if he was stranded somewhere, waiting on three women to go shopping. But this was different; there was a whole store full of fireworks. The men piled out of the car and were inside before the girls could even back out. LW was the last to enter, and he almost collided into the backs of his two cousins. They were just standing there, mouths hanging open.

"What's wrong with you two?" he asked. Then he looked into the store. The walls were wrapped in fishing rods, lures, and nets. The back of the store was reserved for bait. Several tanks with aerators sat on the floor, and four refrigerators hummed against the wall. The front door to the bait area was dominated by eight long tables, each about three feet in width. They were stacked solid with every kind of fireworks known to man, and then some. Cherry bombs in assorted colors and sizes, dozens of different kinds of bottle rockets, and Roman candles sat enticingly on display.

"By God, we've found the holy grail of fireworks stores," Billy said in awe. Henry and LW were still too stunned to reply. LW looked at a sign that read "Bottle rockets a dime a dozen." Another sign offered cherry bombs at the same price. He picked up three dozen bottle rockets and a dozen cherry bombs. Finding a bag left for the purpose, he stuffed his purchases inside.

An hour later, LW looked up to see Doris standing beside him. She was admiring some sparklers. She grabbed a dozen and dropped them into LW's bag. Then she got another handful and dropped them in, too.

"Hey, how much are you going to spend on this stuff?" LW asked in a indignant tone.

"As much as you are if you don't shut up," she replied sweetly. LW was about to reply and then thought better of it.

"Make sure you purchase some big rockets. We want a good show," she said as she slipped another dozen sparklers into his bag. LW watched her walk out of the store and shook his head. Without another word, he walked over to the big rockets and began to browse through them.

Katy was doing everything she could to keep from laughing out loud. She covered her mouth and followed Doris out the door. LW soon forgot about the encounter, as his attention was drawn to an eight-cylinder rocket launcher. It boasted that it shot forty rockets up hundreds of feet into the air.

"Billy, you and Henry buy the main show. I've got the grand finale." LW struggled to get his purchases back to the counter. They filled the trunk with fireworks before returning to the beach.

That evening, the three of them prepared for the display. The girls and LW Sr. gathered out on the deck to enjoy the show. It started with bottle rockets and cherry bombs, but as darkness fell, they moved to the more exciting fare. Billy began lighting off his rockets. Blue and red explosions filled the sky. These were joined by Roman candles, their fireballs racing up with a solid yellow glow. LW Sr. was admiring the fireworks while munching on fried trout and redfish, leftovers from their evening meal. He had just reached for his beer when a bottle rocket shot up and over the balcony. He ducked as it flew past his head and exploded a mere three feet away.

"Hey, you boys watch where you shoot those things. Someone could get hurt," he shouted angrily. He failed to see the smoking bundle of black cats that came bouncing over the rail. The bottle rocket had been the distraction. He grumbled about his spilled beer and then sat back down. His rear end had just touched down when the black cats went off. He jumped up and sent his beer flying into the corner. The women were holding their ears and yelling at their attackers. The roar from the firecrackers was deafening, and smoke filled the balcony. Unable to defend themselves, they retreated to the safety of the house. By the time the last black cat blew itself into oblivion, the balcony was devoid of life. The girls swore vengeance on the transgressor, though they weren't specific in their allegations.

LW Sr. had no doubts about the identity of the culprit. He stormed down the stairs and, spotting his intended prey, he launched into an attack.

LW was well prepared for this development. With his back to the sea, he was confident in his ability to fall back. But given the adversary, he saw little reason to retreat. He also happened to be holding a freshly lit Roman candle. He waited for his father to clear the house, and then he swung the tube into his father's path.

Too late to avoid an impact, LW Sr. tried to stop. The first ball of fire slammed into his chest. He began running in circles as the darkness around him was lit up with balls of fire. He somehow avoided the majority of them, but the ones that hit managed to singe hair and clothes.

LW had already secured a fresh tube and was preparing to light it when a string of explosions ripped the ground around his feet. He backpedaled to safety and turned to find Henry throwing black cats and cherry bombs. LW turned his Roman candle in his cousin's direction. Henry did not give ground, and in the back of LW's mind, warning bells sounded. LW ducked and finally began his retreat. It was a good thing he did, because a loud noise and a bright light flew through the spot his head had just occupied. He saw Billy loading another bottle rocket, and from the corner of his eye, he could see that his father had recovered. Embattled on three sides, he did what any old navy man would; he retreated to the dark waters of the open ocean. He did manage to grab a spare Roman candle and a handful of bottle rockets on his way out.

His father's thirst for revenge was driving him straight at his beleaguered son. Stopping only to grab some cherry bombs, he continued after the distant figure. Billy circled down the beach and closed off any escape. Henry, seeing his cousin's action and observing that his uncle preferred a direct assault, moved in on LW's right. Fireworks lit the night sky, reminding Tabby of a battle seen at a distance. Indeed it was a battle and one that had but a single possible outcome. LW had fired off the last Roman candle and was now forced deeper into the water. The water gave him some protection but came at a high price. He lit his first bottle rocket, and lacking any way to guide it, he threw it in the direction of his father. He cried out in frustration as the rocket soared up and away from his father. LW Sr. started throwing his cherry bombs. Like grenades, they needed no further guidance. Soon the water around him began to boil. The explosive power of the small firecrackers was impressive on land; underwater, they were downright dangerous.

Doris stood on the recently reoccupied balcony, watching as her husband was slowly forced away from the beach. She was as mad as anyone about the unprovoked attack, but she felt a little sadness at the hopeless situation her husband now found himself in. She did not hear Katy come up beside her.

"Reminds you of a story doesn't it?" Katy said.

"What do you mean?" Doris questioned.

"You know, the one about that big German battleship that was surrounded by smaller ships. They pounded on it until it was finally beat." The other women had joined them and stood watching the onslaught.

"Have they always fought like this?" Tabby inquired.

"Since before they could walk. Though usually LW Sr. stays neutral," LW's mother stated disgustedly.

LW was getting worn out. He was now in neck-deep water, and his fireworks were useless. The bottle rockets were skimming the top of the water and coming in fast. He decided to submerge and swim parallel to the shoreline. He disappeared under the water just as a cherry bomb hit a foot away. It happened to be the last in his father's arsenal. The small firecracker sunk slowly and was carried by the wave action to within six inches of the side of LW's head. When it detonated, LW felt a massive pop in each ear and incredible pain. He began to feel nauseous. The world was spinning out of control. Racked with pain, he fought to stay above the surface. Luckily, his feet found the sand and he struggled forward.

His father spotted him and moved in for the kill. As he got closer, he noticed the strange look written upon his son's face. His first thought was that a shark had bitten him. Without hesitation, he swam out and grabbed LW by the arm. Practically carrying LW, he waded towards the beach. He called out for Billy and Henry to help him. They quickly responded and helped get their cousin ashore. They searched his body for obvious signs of trauma. Finding none, they began to question him. He totally ignored them but then rolled his head to the side. They all saw the blood. Henry yelled for Tabby to assist him as they began to panic. They simply could not find the wound they knew was there.

All four women came running up. Tabby quickly knelt beside LW and began to probe his head. She ordered them to carry him inside so she could get a look at him under the lights. LW helped her out by refusing to remove his hands from his ears. The blood ran through his fingers and down his face.

After getting a good look at him in the house, Tabby said, "He has blown his eardrums. Probably has a concussion, too."

"How could that happen?" his mother asked.

"Probably from a firecracker," Tabby said accusingly.

"LW, can you hear me?" his father yelled.

"No, he can't hear you; he lost his eardrums," Tabby replied angrily.

"Let's take him to the doctor," Doris said with tears running down her cheeks.

"I'll drive," said LW Sr. as he headed out the door.

The couples loaded up LW and then watched as his parents and Doris drove off. After a while, Henry and Billy went back to lighting off firecrackers. They were both too freshly removed from the battlefield to be too upset about an injured comrade.

The entire way to the hospital, LW Sr. apologized to LW. Annie's face looked like it was carved out of stone. She listened to her husband and wondered if he really thought LW could hear him. She spent the next two hours alternating between comforting her son and comforting her husband. She was not really angry at LW Sr. LW had brought this on himself. Given that he and his cousins had been in combat, they should have known the consequences of playing with explosives, even on a small scale. But her husband's continued apologies were driving her nuts. LW was not on death's door, and after living so long with the possibility that at any day he could be, she was hardened to the smaller pains of life. When LW came out wrapped in gauze from ear to ear, she couldn't contain her laughter. Her son just glared and walked, unsteadily, out to the car.

The next morning, everyone chipped in to help clean and pack up. LW, though still in pain, tried to do his part. Nobody felt anything but pity for him now. The funny side of the previous evening's events were overshadowed by LW's suffering.

The trip home was a long and quiet one. The group was simply worn out. LW had taken some pain pills and was pretty much comatose. Doris, too, was tired and spent most of the trip sleeping. Her mother-in-law alternated driving with her husband so he would not fall asleep again. Finally, the four-day holiday was over and everyone could get back to their lives.

LW walked into the kitchen, having just got home from work, and hugged Doris. He reached for her hand and guided her outside.

"What are you doing?"

"Just get in the car. Trust me," he said with a smile.

"Okay," she said with some concern in her voice. LW's surprises could sometimes be a little strange, so she was not shocked when he drove north out of town and turned off on a dirt road. He pulled up to a grassy stretch of land. Small red flags could be seen running in straight lines, crisscrossing each other at regular intervals.

"Well, what do you think?"

"Think about what?"

"Think about our plot of land."

"What do you mean?"

"This whole area is being broken up into a housing unit. I bought us this big corner lot to build on," he stated cheerfully.

Doris was caught completely off guard. Tears started to pool in her eyes, and she looked over the large lot more closely. She threw her arms around him and squeezed.

"So these red flags denote our property line?" she asked.

"Yes, they do. I was thinking of putting the house closer to the front, but that's something we can work out together. Think about it—someday our children are going to be running around right here. Then later on, our grandchildren will hunt Easter eggs right over there." She watched as his eyes got a faraway look and she cried even harder.

LW walked over to where a future backyard would be and turned to his wife. He was shocked by the tears. "What's wrong? Don't you like it?" he asked. She tried to answer but her emotions welled up, choking off her answer. "Look, if you don't like it, I can talk to the owner and see if we can get our money back."

"No, it's just that I am so happy," she choked out.

He felt relief rush through him. He put his arm around her and continued, "I can put a garden in right here, and next to that, the pens to keep my hunting dogs. He continued to point out where different things could go. Then he said, "We can put a swing set right here. Can you imagine our kids playing and running? If you close your eyes, you can almost hear them."

"And if you touch my abdomen, you can almost feel one of them," she said quietly.

"Well, I guess so." He had no idea what she was talking about.

"I mean, in a few months you will feel one," she said a little more straight-forwardly.

"Okay. And if you can imagine a big house right here," he said, trying to move on to a new subject. Doris was really acting peculiar. *Maybe she is sick*, he thought. "Look, maybe we should just go home and talk about this tomorrow."

"No, I think we need to talk about this now," she said.

"Am I missing something here?" he asked.

"Just the fact that your wife is pregnant," she said, frustrated.

LW was blindsided. He looked at his wife like she was crazy.

"I know you heard me. Your ears are working just fine now."

He answered her by picking her up in a bear hug. And just as quickly, he put her back down and apologized. They both began to laugh. He put his arm around her, and they stood staring at the setting sun, standing where, in a short time, their back porch would be. The sun slowly dropped behind the horizon, and night fell on what was left of the great Southern plains.